# Terms & Turns:
# Sex & Submission

## *Book I: Becoming a Good Boy*

## By Jon Zelig

# Write a Review:
# Get a FREE eBook!

Review anything written by Jon, Joy, or Bram Zelig, send me a link to the site on which it's been posted. Let me know your preferred format, and which eBook listed below you are interested in.

**jonzelig@anonymousspeech.com**

### Jon Zelig:

Sold #1: A Femdom Vignette
They Say Payback's A—: A Femdom Revenge Story
To Love, Honor, and Obey: A Femdom Wedding Tale

### Joy Zelig:

Chemical Accidents: An Age Play Tale
The Good Master, Book I: Losing Darla
Yes, Daddy: An Age Play Novella

### Bram Zelig:

Sister No More an Erotic Vampire Romance
Book II: The Truth *Won't* Set You Free

### Zoë Zelig:

Tales from a Long Island Dungeon a BDSM Romance
Book I: A Diamond in the Rough

## Disclaimers

- Readers offended by the explicit description of sexual acts, as well as all those under the age of eighteen—or the "adult content" age threshold under the laws of their own countries or jurisdictions—should not continue reading.
- This story is an explicit and sexually graphic depiction of *power exchange* relationships between characters who are all consenting adults.
- This is *not* a representation of non-consensual sexual practices, which the author does not in any way endorse or condone.
- This is a work of fiction: Any resemblance to real persons, living or dead, is purely coincidental.

# The Zelig Family E-Mail List

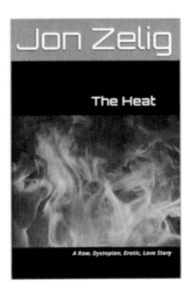

Sign up; get a free PDF of Jon Zelig's *The Heat: A Raw, Dystopian, Erotic, Love Story.*

Receive periodic updates, bonuses, and freebies from Jon, Joy, Bram, and Zöe Zelig.

Your email address will NEVER be revealed, loaned, given, or sold to *any-other-entity* EVER.

Sign up here: **http://eepurl.com/cKUGov**

Let me know: **jonzelig@anonymousspeech.com**

I'll send the free book.

Thanks!

JZ

# The Zelig Family

*Weird genetics? Something in the water? Odd family dynamics?* Whatever it is . . . The Zeligs *do* seem to be a little . . . erotically obsessed. But each one in their own particular way:

***Bram Zelig*** skews toward Paranormal Romance & Erotica.

***Jon Zelig*** does Femdom, often w/ elements of age play, cuckolding & male chastity.

***Joy Zelig***—Jon's twin and mirror image—does more Maledom.

***Zoë Zelig*** is softer; BDSM, Maledom oriented, but more romantic, something of a *Fifty Shades of Grey*-inflected focus on wealth & power.

Their characters tend to love one another and they have an ongoing interest in the moral underpinnings of power exchange: What's consent, where are the lines, who gets to judge—sexually or emotionally? What's public and what's private? When do pain and pleasure shade into damage?

They're trying to do what we all try to do: just . . . make it work.

www.amazon.com/author/bramzelig
www.amazon.com/author/jonzelig
www.amazon.com/author/joyzelig
www.amazon.com/author/zoezelig

# Table of Contents

*Terms & Turns: Sex & Submission*
*Book I: Becoming a Good Boy*

## Part I: Awakening

Chapter One: Awakening     1
Chapter Two: Surrender     13
Chapter Three: Protection     19

## Part II:  Changes

Chapter Four: Saturday Afternoon     25
Chapter Five: Changes     33
Chapter Six: Helping Mommy     45
Chapter Seven: Hints     53

## Part III:  Fault Lines

Chapter Eight: Fridays     61
Chapter Nine: Fault Lines     73
Chapter Ten: Mommy's Boyfriend     79

## Part IV:  Letting Go

Chapter Eleven: Letting Go     85
Chapter Twelve: Apologizing to Mrs. Garber     89
Chapter Thirteen: Mommy Makes a Popsicle     97

## Part V:  After

Chapter Fourteen: The Nice Man     113
Chapter Fifteen: After     119

BONUS Chapter!
An Excerpt from Jon Zelig's:
*The Heat*     125

The Zelig Family                    133

Meet Jon Zelig                      135
Work by Jon Zelig                   137
Connect with Jon Zelig              143

Meet Joy Zelig                      145
Work by Joy Zelig                   147

Meet Bram Zelig                     151
Work by Bram Zelig                  153

Meet Zoë Zelig                      155
Work by Zoë Zelig                   157

Email List                          159
FREE Book!                          161

Reviews                             163

# Part I: Awakening

# Chapter One: Awakening

*"Get up!"*

I woke up groggy and confused, struggling to pull myself free from the tangle of my dreams, the clock on the night table flashing 3:35 a.m., the Friday night—Saturday morning—of a three-day weekend, Monday off.

"Up!" my wife said again, sharply. "Downstairs. *Now.*"

Stumbling to my feet, I reached for the robe hanging on the back of the bedroom door, moving to comply though I couldn't fathom what was going on.

*"No!"* she said, with the vehemence and the tone you would use to give an order to a dog.

She slapped my face, quickly and with some force.

I hadn't had time to register whether or not I had an erection when I stood up; my eyes widened in shock, my jaw dropped, I blinked; a surge of blood—unanticipated, intense, and mortifying—made my cock visibly twitch.

She noted this with a curt nod and a pursing of her lips, held my eyes for a long moment, then turned on her heel and walked down the stairs.

Neither of us had ever hit the other.

I didn't understand, neither what she had done nor the combination of my reactions: the erection and my

1

passivity and compliance. It was confusing of course, and the context fogged things further; in the bright light of day, I might have slapped her in return, or protested or resisted or asked questions. We'd been married for more than a decade, together for even longer. Things were going well, we were happy—as far as I knew up to that point.

There wasn't any bleeding but surely there would be a bruise. I followed her in a numb daze, feeling as if I were simultaneously watching this happen to someone else.

She looked crisp and businesslike: the lacy trim of an almost translucent bra visible beneath a thin white silk blouse, a black pencil skirt with a side zipper, black stockings and spike heels, her hair neatly and tightly pinned up, makeup subtle but complete, the faint aroma of the perfume I favored.

"Stand *there*," she said, pointed to the center of the living room carpet, settling herself on the couch with precision, crossing one knee over the other, folding her hands in her lap.

My mouth was dry and I could feel my forehead, twitching in perplexity, begin to sheen with perspiration; my cheek burned where she had slapped me; the room was warm but my arms were cold; my hard-on undiminished, the throbbing painful and embarrassing, a physiological confession and betrayal.

I did as she told me.

At first I rested my hands on the fronts of my thighs. Then I clasped them together behind my back. Then I returned them to their original position. I didn't know how to stand and I didn't know where to look. Focusing on these details was easier than trying to take in the whole of what was happening, what felt like a tilting, a violation, of reality.

"You've been masturbating," she said, a flat statement of fact with soft undertones of amusement and disapproval. "And you've been watching porn."

I didn't think there was really anything wrong with either of those activities, but—still half-asleep, nude, hard, actually *called on the carpet*—I couldn't quite fumble out any kind of response before she added, her voice soft and low but sharp, "You did *not* have my permission to do those things."

She stood up, walked slowly toward me until we were nearly toe to toe; we're almost the same height.

I felt her fingernails—a light, sharp, asymmetric circle—constrict to just graze the head of my cock, then stop, the feeling that of a small swarm of bees menacing but not following through on the threat.

She was again looking unblinkingly into my eyes. Her voice got even softer, a breathy growl.

"*Mistress Mommy* finds that *very* disappointing."

The title she had given herself made my stomach lurch and my hard-on twitch.

I was stunned, enthralled—disgusted with and ashamed of the part of me excited by what she had said—felt dizzy, wanted to respond but couldn't find the right words.

"I want you to apologize," she said, her hand moving lower, firmly grasping my balls.

"I'm sorry I . . . *did* that?" I managed, feeling like there was a kind of dream logic that it was important for me to follow.

She squeezed with enough force to make one of my knees flex involuntarily. I gasped in pain, unable to pull away.

"I'm sorry. *Mistress.* Mommy," she said.

"I'm sorry Mistress Mommy," I repeated hurriedly.

" . . . that I played with my *wee-wee.* . ."

"*What?*"

She squeezed even harder the second time and both knees almost went.

"*Jesus!* That I played with my wee-wee. . ."

3

"Without your permission. . ."

" . . . without your permission."

She let go and I groaned in relief, her fingers gliding back up to lightly encircle the head of my cock again.

"There!" she cooed in my ear, her lips grazing my neck. "*That* wasn't so difficult was it?"

"No. . ." seemed to be the right answer, but I felt her hand start to descend again. "No Mistress Mommy," I added quickly and her nails instead resumed their tantalizing contact.

"Such a *very* good boy," she breathed into my ear. "And still *so* hard," she observed with something that sounded like both satisfaction and a little derision.

She let her hand drop and walked slowly around me, as though inspecting a statue, or a horse she was considering buying, fingertips lightly grazing my belly, my hip; she came to a stop behind me, a single finger barely touching the cleft at the top of my buttocks.

I could feel the silk of her blouse caress my back; she had one foot a little forward, slightly parting my legs, the sleek nylon of her stocking against my calf, the taut smooth fabric of her skirt on the back of my thigh—her chin brushing but not quite resting on my shoulder.

"Apologizing is a good start," she said, the words a warm, moist rush in my ear. "There is still the matter of punishment." She shook her head quickly back and forth and giggled, her nose in my hair. "And—of course—*prevention.*"

We had played games before.

She had always been more cooperative than enthusiastic, usually more comfortable as a bottom than as a top, tended, as a matter of tone, toward tolerant rather than intense. Her attitude fit her approach to negotiating things like which one of us chose a restaurant or a weekend movie. She wanted to be fair, let me have my menu choices as long as she got hers in similar measure—and as long as I didn't try to order anything *too* weird.

I don't know how to explain what's wrong with *me*.

Sex to her, it had seemed to me—as perhaps it is for most people—had always been like alcohol to a social drinker: that mellow and satisfying single glass of wine after work; the occasional weekend binge; perhaps every few years things get out of control at a wild party, leaving you a little hung over and sheepish, but with an odd, guilt-tinged sense of accomplishment.

I want to be *annihilated*.

I want to mainline heroin and soar out of my body—out of my mind, too, for that matter. Call me a switch. It's almost the same rush whether the drug is absolute power or absolute powerlessness.

Power or terror, pleasure or pain, it's the cold wave of an adrenalin rush, the warm ocean of a dopamine high. It's why some people skydive, I guess.

The problem with being the top is that you have to keep enough of your wits about you to plan and arrange, you can't fully escape—your body, your mind, your reality—in the same way. If you're the bottom, all you have to do is surrender. If your partner is serious, she incinerates any thought in your head but the trembling anticipation of what might happen next.

I don't know what had happened.

She seemed serious.

This came home to me harder than the face slap when she giggled.

She had played stern before, the dominant mistress. But it had always been a role, someone else's script—mine I guess, in some form or other. The laughter was new, though, and it was genuine—spontaneous pleasure at what she was doing to me, who she was making me, who she was making herself.

Our role playing had always felt, had always been, bounded to some degree, a set of agreements and scenarios that went just to the edge.

Waking me up at three in the morning felt like she had pushed me over the edge, into free fall, real fear, real humiliation, a mouse paralyzed in terror before a snake, mesmerized by my own helplessness, not even a remote possibility that I could escape, little likelihood that I would survive, my only option compliance, dazed but fervent, undergirded by a chilling sense of futility: the mouse has no power before the snake; the child has no power before the mother.

"You *will* be punished," she said again, pressing herself fully against my back, her hands suddenly tight on the fronts of my thighs; she briefly kissed, then sucked, then bit my neck—*hard.*

I jumped and cried out; she held fast, her pelvis grinding against my ass for a moment as I tried to squirm away; her fingers arched, nails against my flesh, in implicit threat, and I froze.

She let one hand drop away for a second, then it was back; I looked down to see her encircle my cock, thumbs above and at the base of the shaft, index fingers below and behind my balls. She had looped a black ribbon, silky and soft, below; crossing the ends over one another at the top, she pulled them tight, the blood in my cock trapped, my balls now a single taut pouch. A second loop and another tightening; then the fast looping and binding at the bottom of the shaft, above my balls.

"But we will not have any accidents. Will we?"

"No. . ."

She flicked the bound package of my balls with her index finger and I saw stars before managing to stammer out, "No, Mistress Mommy."

"*Ohh,*" she cooed, hugging me hard from behind, her lips nuzzling my neck.

"Such a *good* boy! Now thank me for saving your *cummies* for you."

"Thank you for saving my . . . *cummies,* Mistress Mommy?" I managed uncertainly. It was as though I were getting a crash course in a new language, spoken in a country I had never visited before. Except, of course, it was maternal language—heightened, sexualized.

"Over the arm of the couch," she said, pointing, her voice once again flat and directive.

I scuttled to the couch quickly, made to kneel facing one of the ends, but she said no.

"Stand," she said. "Bend at the waist, so your head is on the arm. Reach back and hold your bottom open for me."

She caressed the small of my back, trailed her fingers up my spine, tousled my hair, paced back and forth in front of me slowly for a moment, rubbing her palm with the back of a wooden hair brush only a little smaller than a paperback book.

Where had *that* come from?

I watched this from the corner of my eye, head down, intent on the patterns embroidered on the couch pillows.

She gave a long thoughtful purring sound—deep but lilting—which chilled me even more than her giggling had, the notes of pleasure in it both obvious and somehow primal.

A finger under my chin, she pushed up to make me meet her gaze, said nothing for a few moments.

"This is going to hurt," she said. "It's going to hurt *a lot*, and," she entwined the fingers of her right hand in my hair, wrenched my head to an angle, brought her cheek against mine and spoke this time directly into my ear, "thinking about that has made Mistress Mommy very, *very* wet. Thinking about what I'm going to do to you, how I'm going to do it, thinking about how I am going to make you—" that purr again, ending in something of a sigh, the

7

sound rising, becoming a little more breathy, "my *utterly* helpless. Good. Little. Boy."

Without letting go of my hair, she sat down on the couch, pulling my head down even further as she did. I almost stumbled; the only thing that stopped me was my chest coming to rest on the arm of the sofa. I stood with my feet slightly apart, my hands behind me, holding the cheeks of my ass apart as she had instructed, bent at the waist, the side of my face now mashed against the front of her skirt.

My back hurt; the muscles in my thighs twitched; the taut and sensitive skin of my bound cock and balls rubbed painfully against the weave of the upholstery.

"Can you *smell* how wet Mommy is?"

I croaked that I could.

I could feel the damp heat, smell her briny and sweet scent, layered on the perfume, the leather of her shoes, the laundry chemicals on her clothing, the shampoo in her hair, the sharp note of her perspiration; she wore no deodorant.

The fingers of one hand remained painfully entwined in my hair, while those of the other gently traced across the upturned half of my face, my nose, my eyebrow, my ear. She tickled my lips with her thumbnail, pushed gently through, then past my teeth and into my mouth—all the way, until she was stopped not by any resistance on my part but by the webbing with her index finger.

I was sucking her thumb.

"That's right," she cooed, "and you keep holding your ass open for me, because" she lowered her voice to a whisper, "I am going to violate. Every. Part. Of. Your. Body. It won't *be* yours anymore."

I felt a sustained tremor of anticipation and couldn't tell how much of it was the thrum of power through her body, how much a shudder of anticipation through mine, an amalgam of fear, exhaustion, and excitement.

8

Again, I was confused, mortified, and frozen.

"You really didn't understand," she said thoughtfully. "And—no—I didn't either. I thought you wanted boots and leather and whips but really, *really,* you want to go back *just* to that edge and be kept there—when you were *about* to go from being a little boy to a big boy, when you were *about* to break free from Mommy but couldn't *quite* do it, when you began to realize that getting hard *meant* something, but you weren't sure exactly *what.*"

"Eleven or twelve, is that how old you really are?" she mused. "Your voice just beginning to crack—which is *so* embarrassing!—just a few strands of that confusing, icky pubic hair? You think you want to be a big boy but Mommy wants to keep you for herself, safe and sweet. And you try so hard, don't you? *So* hard, but Mommy is just too powerful. *Which feels terrible!* Which feels *wonderful.*"

"And you were remembering things," she continued, her voice getting husky. "That when your head only came up to Mommy's waist and you ran up and put your arms around her—hugging her beautiful, soft, comforting bottom—when she pressed you to her skirt, you smelled something, didn't you? Something you weren't supposed to smell. That sometimes she just couldn't find a washcloth so she soaped your wee-wee with her hands, making sure she got you very, *very* clean. Sometimes that made you hard, didn't it? And when you had a fever and Mommy took your temperature, she was always very gentle, wasn't she? She used *plenty* of Vaseline, took such a *long* time opening up your little bottom for the thermometer, even though you were so hot and drowsy and squirming, and your little wee-wee got hard again against the sheets."

She leaned over, her thumb still in my mouth and kissed my cheek softly.

"You didn't know that was bad, did you? It was just confusing. Mommy did things to your body; Mommy took care of her little boy; and your body did those *disgusting*," she yanked my hair briefly and I moaned, her thumb preventing me from crying out, "those disgusting things that," she lowered her voice to a whisper again, "felt *so* good, so *terribly* good."

She leaned over, this time shaking her head back and forth so that her nose grazed my face as she giggled again.

"It was confusing, very confusing, wasn't it? You knew those things were bad but they made you feel good. And *such* shame! All Mommy wanted to do was take care of you, and *that's* how you responded?"

The thumb in my mouth prevented me from answering.

"But it's okay now," she continued. "I understand; I do. You're going to be Mistress Mommy's little boy now, and I'm going to take care of you and take care of your wee-wee. You don't have to worry; you won't be responsible. All of the *terrible* things I'm going to do," I felt her shiver as she said that, with an intensity that might almost have been mistaken for a small, fast orgasm, "you won't be able to stop them, no; so it won't be your fault. Mistress Mommy will take absolute control of her little boy."

"But first you need to be punished," she said, her voice suddenly brisk again. "And this *is* going to hurt."

She stood up abruptly, pulling her thumb from my mouth with a pop that was almost audible, moved behind me, leaned over quickly to kiss the small of my back, gently stroking my buttocks with the cold smooth grain of the wooden hair brush.

"It will be okay," she said, soothingly. "I'm going to hurt you, but it will be okay. As long as you obey me absolutely, I'm going to free you from all of those bad, guilty, big boy problems. You'll be my happy little boy; I promise. Now ask Mistress Mommy to punish you."

I was barely able to fight off the urge to cry, gave a single sob—of gratitude or fear or disgust or confusion, of desire or pain or relief or incredulity—and did as I had been told.

## Chapter Two: Surrender

The spanking hurt.

But when it was over she didn't have to prompt me to thank her for my punishment.

My ass hurt terribly, it was hot, it had to be bright red, but my gratitude was real.

I felt a tremendous and pervasive relief that I couldn't explain to myself.

It didn't feel personal—like something she had done to me—it was larger than that: the astonishment—the *awe*—one might feel at the passing of a brief, violent, summer storm; a curtain yanked back, the sky suddenly clear and unmarred blue, the sun warm but not hot, the air sweet and clear, the anger of the lightning and the thunder almost instantly gone.

"Very good!" she said. "You took your spanking *very* well and I'm proud of you. What a *good* little boy!"

I murmured another thanks in response.

"You can stand up now, but keep your feet apart and your hands holding open your bottom."

I complied, not sure where to look. I was sure my face was red, too.

I looked back at the middle of the living room carpet, where I had been standing, just a few minutes before; my eyes flickered across the coffee table in front of the couch, a rosewood box there, the cover carved and inlaid with ivory in the pattern of a bouquet of tulips—that was new; I looked furtively at her face for a moment and saw that she was flushed as well, from exertion or in triumph, eyes glittering, lips set in a tight, satisfied smile, her nipples visibly erect through the double—albeit sheer—layers of her blouse and filmy bra.

"Eyes down," she said softly.

She walked slowly to the coffee table. From the corner of my eye, I could see her bend briefly, open the rosewood box, take something out, close the lid again.

I was still off to the side, facing the arm of the couch over which she had made me lean while she punished me.

"Turn," she said quietly—having stalked over to me, the swish of her nylons barely audible—and we were face to face. "You may look at my hands."

Raising my eyes, I saw that she held a transparent medical exam glove and a tube of lubricant.

"Keep looking," she murmured, fitting the glove onto her right hand, tugging on each finger, slowly, methodically, making sure it was tight, pulling the glove back at her wrist, flicking open the cap of the tube of lubricant with her thumb and squeezing a dollop onto the middle finger of her gloved hand, using the thumb and forefinger of the other hand, as if delicately masturbating a pencil, to coat first it, then her ring finger, then her index finger—all of them—completely, from palm to tip.

I couldn't breathe properly.

Or quietly.

"*Now* you may look me in the eyes."

I didn't want to, hanging my head instead and concentrating on her feet, the strappy high heels, the smoky black stockings.

14

"But, *no*— I don't. . ." I started.  But stating a desire— asking for, let alone demanding, anything—was somehow terrifying, impossible.  "It isn't—"

"*Fair?*" she put in when I hesitated, and I nodded in frustrated mortification.

She leaned over to put the tube down on the coffee table, her blouse opening briefly.  Concealed only by the sheer bra, the fabric like cellophane, with just the slightest tinge of beige, I could see that—in addition to the prominence of her nipples—her areolas had darkened, crinkled, and tightened.  That was rare, something that only happened when she was in a particularly intense and extended state of arousal.

The sharp threat of her nails once again encircled the red and bulging head of my bound cock, flexing for a quick moment so I felt just a brief kiss of the pain she could cause by squeezing, opening again, her touch feathery with a hint of potential pleasure.  She dropped the hand to my balls but just held them as if judging their weight or value for a second, though the black silk ribbon that bound both them and my cock meant that they couldn't hang freely.

She brought her ungloved hand up to my face, pressed her slightly slick index finger under my chin and brought my head up until I was forced to look into her eyes.

"You failed to use the proper form of address just now," she said icily.

"But that's alright," she added quickly, just brushing my cheek with her lips.  "Mistress Mommy sometimes forgives little boys when they've mostly been good. *Sometimes*.  Not often."

I tried to nod, but the finger under my chin would not permit this.

"It's *not* fair," she said.  "You did what you were told to do.  Mommy got you out of bed in the middle of the night.  She tied up your wee-wee!  She spanked you *very* hard, didn't she?  And you took it very well, you did."

15

Again I couldn't nod.

"And now she *is* going to violate your bottom. She *is*," her voice had the calm, logical force of maternal inevitability. "This is not a discussion and it is not a negotiation. It's not—" I averted my eyes for a second and her voice rose, more in intensity than in volume, until I once again returned her gaze as steadily as I could manage. "It's not a game. It doesn't start and stop when *you* want and you don't make the rules. And, no," she dropped the hand that had been under my chin back down to grip my balls again, her eyes warning me not to look away, "it's *not* fair."

Moving the gloved hand through my legs, below and behind, she quickly and easily slipped her slick middle finger between my buttocks, bringing it just into contact with my anus, applying enough pressure to threaten but not to penetrate.

I couldn't hold back a strangled whining sound of fear and frustration.

Her grip on my balls was firm but not quite painful, the finger at my anus moving almost imperceptibly, a sort of gentle, teasing tickle; she brought her face to mine and began giving me breathy little kisses on my cheeks, my chin, my forehead, my neck.

"*Shhh, shhh, shhh. . .*" as you might calm a nervous child or soothe a balky horse.

I closed my eyes, breathing in her scent, her hair, her perfume.

"The problem," she said huskily, as she continued to kiss me, "isn't that it hurts. No."

She brought her lips to mine for the first time that night, kissed and nibbled at them gently, then bit my lower lip hard—only her hand on my balls keeping me from moving back, which would have impaled me on her finger.

"The problem," she continued, now talking as if directly to my mouth, her tongue gently laving my lips,

16

slowly beginning to part them, to penetrate, "isn't that you *don't* want this."

She pulled back and looked directly into my eyes again.

"The problem is that you *do* want this," she said, not quite with anger but with intensity. "*That's* the problem. But that's okay," she said hurriedly, her voice soft again, as she returned to kissing my mouth, harder now. "Yes it is. Because *you don't have a choice.* No. It is very important—" she paused, then repeated, "*very* important for you to understand this. Mommy *will* violate your bottom, Mommy *will* punish you, Mommy can do absolutely anything she wants to her little boy—to any and every part of his body," she said with a soft note of appreciative wonder in her voice, "any time she wants to."

I closed my eyes and nodded quickly, trying not to cry, whether in relief or in fear, shame or desire.

"Ask," she breathed the word on my face, so softly I almost couldn't hear.

"Please Mistress Mommy," I started, my breathing a little uneven. "Please violate my bottom."

"Oh, *such* a good little boy!" she cried as she plunged her finger in up to the second knuckle, her tongue simultaneously thrusting, hard and deep, into my mouth.

She moved even closer, shifted a little to the side, so that my thigh was between her legs, pressed against me tightly, gyrating her hips just a little, moving very slowly as if speed might hurt one or both of us, as if she did not trust herself to go any faster, as if she understood the potentially dangerous intensity of what she was unleashing in herself.

She stopped kissing me for a moment but pulled her face back almost not at all, so that we were just about nose to nose. "And how many fingers should Mistress Mommy use to violate her little boy's bottom?" she asked, her voice hoarse, her breathing ragged.

17

"Mommy should—" I fumbled in a dazed panic as she pulsed her finger urgently in and out, fully inside me now as deep as she could go.  I felt like a puppet, wholly in her control; it felt like she could simply reach in and stroke my heart, which was hammering wildly.  "Mistress Mommy should do anything she wants to me," I managed to choke out.

She gave a long, loud, moan of approval at that, spasming against my leg repeatedly and came; her knees buckled and I had to hold her up.

"I have such a *good* little boy," she moaned over and over, riding my leg and the waves of her own pleasure. "Yes, *such* a good little boy."

Her hands flexed as if with palsy, the finger in my ass joined by a second, making me dance in response, the hand gripping my balls pulsing little flashes of shimmering pain through my throbbing cock, alloyed with a pleasure that was not quite enough to cancel it out.

I wouldn't have been able to come anyway.

The silk ribbon tight around my cock and balls, Mommy had made sure to keep my cummies safe.

## Chapter Three: Protection

The face in the mirror, in the bahroom—where my wife had sent me to "freshen up," though the binding of my cock meant that I couldn't pee—looked shell-shocked.

It was a look as much of wonderment as it was of fear or pleasure or pain, the wide-eyed shock of a little boy. Five a.m. and it didn't seem possible that I had been awake for almost an hour and a half.

What had happened didn't seem possible either.

My cock and balls, still bound with that black silk ribbon, were both a deep shade of red. My balls throbbed, the tip of my cock burned, the shaft felt a little numb.

In the living room—I imagined—my wife sat on the couch, placidly sipping from a mug: half coffee, half Irish whiskey, just a jot of sugar and cinnamon, a fast froth of steamed milk to top it. Her instructions had been quite precise.

"Make me a nice cappuccino," she'd started with. "Then you may go freshen up a little. More to do when you come back," she'd said brightly, closing her eyes and giving a drowsy sigh before repeating dreamily, "*so* much more."

When I returned, she looked refreshed.

"So you've *seen*," she said slowly, as if deep in thought, sitting in the middle of the couch, after having directed me to kneel on the living room carpet, "that Mistress Mommy has a toy chest for you."

The rosewood box, something between the size of a cigar box and a briefcase, sat on the coffee table that separated us.

I told her, in satisfactory fashion, that I had.

She closed her eyes for a moment, seemed lost in thought.

"And Mommy had lube in there for your little bottom, didn't she?"

My throat was too dry to answer, though it was clear that was what was required.

She opened her eyes and transfixed me.

"*Didn't she?*" the phrase then a straightforward demand to which I acquiesced.

"And that nice glove," she continued, "because you wouldn't want your nasty little bottom to soil Mommy's fingers?"

"No, Mistress Mommy," I murmured in answer.

"What *else* do you think is in your toy chest?" this time a low, wicked, whisper, that froze me; I couldn't guess what the right answer was.

*Were there things I was supposed to know about, and to ask for?*

*Were there things I might come up with on my own in error?*

*Would they result in punishment or would she use them against me in some other way?*

"I don't know . . . Mistress Mommy," I mumbled, and hung my head in confusion and surrender.

"You don't *know!?*" she said brightly, as if in surprise, rising from the couch and skirting the coffee table to stand over me, cupping my chin in her palm and raising me face to look at her. "Oh, I think you *do!* But let's open it

20

together and see!" as if we were going on some kind of mutual adventure.

*What would we find?*

"There!" she said, opening the box and pulling something out, holding it in front of my face, stroking my cheek with it, poking it playfully at my lips. "You know what *this* is for, don't you?"

She didn't just know that I had been looking at porn.

She knew, in some detail, exactly what *kind* of porn: dangling in front of my face was a clear neoprene chastity cage.

Turning and bending to the box again, she pulled something else out.

*"Look!"* she said, as if in happy surprise, holding up the small brass padlock, "it's a *set!"*

I hadn't answered her question, hadn't admitted that I knew what it was.

She didn't press me, just looked steadily into my eyes, an occasional twitch at the corners of her mouth suggesting that she was holding back a smile.

Then she scrunched up her face into a thoughtful, mock-scowl.

"Be my good little boy," she said, firmly, "you march right into the kitchen and get us a towel and a bowl of ice. And when you come back," now her face and voice took on a pouty *faux* sympathy, her lips pursed as she nodded, as if in sadness, *"yes,* we're going to ice down your *wee-wee* until it's *very* small, so we can get you . . . properly secured."

21

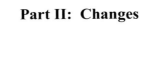

**Part II: Changes**

## Chapter Four: Saturday Afternoon

I resisted waking up for as long as I could.

Then I resisted admitting to myself—or giving any outward sign—that I was awake, eyes resolutely closed, cheek rubbing the pillow, my brow periodically furrowing with effort.

Was one of my cheeks slightly sore? I tried not to notice.

*I'd had a weird, twisted, Freudian dream?*

*My wife had experienced something approaching a psychotic break—and taken me along for the ride?*

*We had played a game that was*—what?—*exciting, disturbing, sick, liberating, deeply erotic, profoundly dangerous?*

She kissed me lightly on my neck, kept her lips just below my ear so that I could feel the soft touch of her breath, spooned against my back, her breasts an irresistible pressure.

She was wearing a nightgown I didn't recognize, plain, white cotton, modest, felt like it went almost to her ankles.

"*Mor*-ning," she said softly, slightly sing-song.

"Hey. . ." I responded, noncommittally, not quite trusting my voice.

It had happened or it hadn't.

And if we talked about it, it would be real.

I shivered and she pressed herself against me more tightly, making a little humming sound of contentment.

"So," she said lightly, "how was your . . . night?"

"It was a little . . . strange," I ventured cautiously.

*"Oh!?"* her tone was of the *who-has-a-boo-boo?* variety, which, of course, fit perfectly.

She snaked her hand down my belly, then beneath, cupped me.

"Aren't you feeling," she asked, her voice happy, calm, light, just a hint of teasing, *"secure?"*

It was there.

In her hand.

Binding and restraining my cock.

*It had happened.*

Breathing was complicated; speech was impossible.

"So *that* was really kind of weird, huh?" a quizzical tone, as if we were talking about an odd TV show we had seen the night before. "Scary, really, but maybe exciting, too—which might be even *more* scary?"

I managed an affirmative noise.

"Because if that really turned you on—if it turned bo*th of us* on—maybe it's a little . . . *twisted?"*

"Yeah. . ." I breathed softly.

"Mmmm," she made that little hum of thoughtful contentment again. "But it *did* really turn you on, didn't it?" Not waiting for a response, "and it turned me on, *too*, which," I felt *her* shiver against *me*, a little thrum through her body that she couldn't control, "which I'd like to . . . explore a little. Could we do that? *Explore?* It's us, it's just us, why shouldn't we see how we feel if we go a little longer or—a little *further?"*

My tongue felt a little sticky and slow.

Given the things she'd done, what could "further" *possibly* mean?

I felt myself on the edge of something.

Maybe I was about to execute a perfect, beautiful, exhilarating cliff dive; maybe I was about to heedlessly throw myself down onto rocks in the surf.

*Jump?*

Which would I regret more, going forward or holding back?

Would stopping be chickening out or basic mental health?

Would going forward be adventurous or something between sick and stupid?

"What would that mean?" I asked, carefully. "*Exploring?*" knowing almost as I said it what her response would have to be.

"What would you *want* it to mean?"

"Well, there would have to be rules," I said, stalling a little.

"*Rules. . .*" she said—thoughtfully, slowly—as if the concept were somewhat alien and she was trying to digest it.

"Well, okay," she said brightly, as if thinking as she went along, "how about you can say 'stop' whenever you want—"

Was it relief or disappointment that shot through me when she said that?

*Great! We can play this game, turn it on, turn it off.*

"—but if we *stop*, that's it, we're done."

Okay . . . there's a safe word, but it's the nuclear option.

"Okay," I said, gingerly. "That sounds good."

"One thing that's not negotiable, though," she said, squeezing my bound cock. "This stays on as long as I want it on, which—you need to understand—will be almost

27

*always.* I'll let you out to play now and then. I'll clean you and take care of you. But this is mine."

She lowered her hand a little to the tight clump of my balls, hanging below the device, caressed briefly and then squeezed hard enough for me to groan and flinch, a flash of pain and then the mortification of my cock trying to get even harder against the restraint.

"I don't really care about porn and masturbation. But you don't get to dissipate the energy that I want— whenever *you* want—for no good reason. That's not negotiable. Oh!—" as if she had forgotten, "And, of course, you have to eat whatever you shoot."

Of course.

She had gone through the porn I was looking at with a fine-toothed comb. She knew *far* too much about what I *thought* I wanted—or about the images and the ideas that turned me on.

"What about doctor's appointments?" I managed, again realizing as I said it that I was asking a logical question to which she would have a logical response: she was letting me paint myself into a corner.

"Well. . ." she appeared to think about it for a moment. "There *may* be situations where it's necessary to— *briefly*—release you. I think the rule should be that, if I let you out, you have to be accompanied at all times until you are properly secured again."

I mulled that for a moment.

"Does that seem reasonable?" she prompted.

"I *guess* so. . ."

"What else?" she said crisply, as if we were moving through a meeting agenda—she did that well at work, I knew—as if we had already made the core decision—and made it together—and now all that remained was ironing out the small details.

"It's. . ." my voice quavered; getting to the next word was hard, and I fell to a whisper, "it's *humiliating.*"

"That's what you *want*," she said matter-of-factly, "to *really* feel—to *accept*—that you've lost control and that you're doing things because you are being forced, things you wouldn't do on your own, things you wouldn't accept if simply proposed to you, things that you simply have to surrender to. *Nasty things*," she whispered. "Because *you*. Are a bad—*bad. Nasty*. Little. Boy."

And we *both* shivered.

"You don't really want to do those things for a *Leather Goddess,* because a Leather Goddess is cold; and you don't want a nanny, because, in the end, a nanny is just an employee; you don't want diapers, you want early adolescence; and you don't really want to do those things with a wife, either, because you think a wife should be an equal."

She paused for a shuddering breath.

"Your Mistress Mommy won't *be* your mother," she said. "That's *different.* She will be the Good/Bad Mommy who totally controls her little boy, who loves him and disciplines him and liberates him and exploits him for her own selfish pleasure; who keeps him for herself; who manipulates him for his own good. Mommy will protect you from the world and from yourself, and you will *thrill* to the knowledge that *nothing* can protect you from Mommy."

Throwing off the covers, she shimmied and hiked the white cotton nightgown to her waist. Beneath, she wore a pair of large, white, full cut, cotton panties, which reached almost to her navel—also something new and different— a wet spot visible, before she peeled them down, kicked them off, revealing that she had totally shaven her cunt, the lips fully exposed, slick, puffy, and red.

"Feel! *Feel!"* she said, taking my hand and thrusting it between her legs, "how hot and *wet* Mommy's *cunny* gets, just *thinking* about taking care of you, about taking *control* of you and *feel*," she said, squeezing my trapped cock, straining and throbbing ceaselessly now against its little cage, "feel how *desperately* excited the idea of surrendering to Mommy makes *you*, how much your little wee-wee *wants*—how much it *needs*—my control."

I whimpered in agreement as she lightly squeezed my pulsing cock.

"This is . . . *private,*" I managed, my last faint gesture in the direction of negotiation.

"Oh, of course, *of course* it is!" she cried, as she turned me toward her. "*Of course* it's private—*at-least-for-now.*"

She murmured that last clause quickly as she peppered my cheeks and forehead with feathery kisses—but it was perfectly clear—and my stomach lurched at the implication, as she began gently pushing my head down her body.

"Now say 'thank you Mistress Mommy'—" she arrested my progress by snaring one of my earlobes.

"Thank you Mistress Mommy—" I repeated dutifully.

"—'for taking care of your little boy'—"

"—for taking care of your little boy—"

"—'and I promise to be good.'"

"I promise to be good."

"Oh," she moaned at my completion of her litany, resuming the downward pressure on my head, her breathing becoming erratic, "and now you . . . *oh!*" as I found the swollen bud of her clit and strummed it with my tongue, "Now you may *thank* . . . Mommy's . . . cunny. Be my good little boy and *thank* Mommy's cunny," as I sealed my lips over her smooth naked mound and sucked, while still flicking.

"*Be my good little boy, be my good little boy . . . be my . . . be . . . be. . .*"

She descended into muttering and moaning as she wrapped her legs around my neck, her hands frantically fluttering from my hair to my shoulders to my ears, the smooth, slick, swollen wetness of her swallowing me up, becoming my only world.

## Chapter Five: Changes

There was a lot of adjusting, between Saturday and Tuesday when we both had to go back to work, and then into the week itself. More for me—as I felt the foundation of my life fall away beneath me.

I was in a perpetual state of uncertainty and anxiety, about what to do and how to do it, about whether or not I was "getting things right," although it came home to me quickly and repeatedly that there was an odd underlying dynamic that had some useful piece to it: I'd spent most of my adult life worrying about *getting things right*; at least now there was a clear, consistent—loving—controlling authority.

Once I knew how something worked, some piece of our new life, I could relax into it, at least a little.

The more paralyzed I was by *what am I supposed to do?* or angry about *it's not fair*, the worse things were.

The more I gave in to *this is just how it works*, the better I felt.

Being a little boy meant that there was no—grownup, real world—way to fight against a raft of problems, or things that I would normally get upset about, so I had to make peace with them as best I could.

*She* was generally quite self-assured: about what would be done, how it would be done, how things were going to be.

We had never argued a great deal or with problematic intensity.

But what I became aware of—as soon as it stopped—was that a great deal of our emotional energy had gone into a kind of low-level scorekeeping, minor tussling over authority, and the accompanying irritations when either of us *didn't get their way.*

She had always been a self-assured person, clear about what she wanted, open to reasonable discussion. I was surprised by how smoothly and unselfconsciously she switched into simply being in charge.

She told me what to do and I did it: No long, drawn out, carefully modulated discussion; no backwash of compromise or irritation; all kinds of things just took much less time and much less energy.

Of course, I *was* irritated—or confused or outright *frightened*—by some of the things she seemed to simply take for granted would happen.

And while I almost never said anything in complaint—was I helping her keep me churning in a maelstrom of emotion that, in some perverse way, I found reassuring? a balance to the new peace born of acquiescence?—she would often see my upset and preëmpt me, always in the same way: Stroking my cheek, sometimes kissing me softly, talking to me in a tone closer to what one would use with an upset toddler.

"*No*," she would say sweetly and sympathetically, shaking her head, "it *isn't* fair, *is it?*" Then a sigh, as if in resignation at the injustice of the world—with which we would *both* simply have to grapple—and she would usually just walk away.

Or she would make an exaggerated pouty face, as if in imitation of me, then pet my groin affectionately—

34

which I could barely feel through the chastity device whether I was clothed or naked.

"You be my good boy now," she would say, in mock seriousness.

It quickly came to feel Pavlovian.

Work was strange on Tuesday.

*How could it* possibly *have been otherwise?*

I was a little tentative and jumpy. I wasn't used to the chastity device yet, and my constant awareness of it, of how it rubbed against my clothing—*was it visible? could other people see it? weren't there changes in me that were glaringly obvious, as well? no one really seemed to notice*—the cycle I went through as the day went on, briefly forgetting and then being startled back to awareness when I thought of something erotic—almost any part of that long, confusing, and exciting weekend— and progress toward an erection quickly came up against the restraint.

It was physically painful, but there was also a frustrating ping ponging back and forth: between physical discomfort and the erotic charge of the constant reminder of what I had acceded to; between anxiety—that there was something just *deeply,* irredeemably, wrong with me, that people would immediately know and respond to this—and an odd germ of peace and acceptance; between frustration at the length of the day and some relief that I had a little time away from home to think.

The biggest mistake I made was to reflexively accept an offer from a colleague to "catch a quick beer after work."

*Just a little more time and space before I go home; get my bearings,* I thought.

But there were *so* many ways in which I hadn't really thought that through . . .

First off, Jimmy wasn't really a friend. He was just a guy from work. We had a beer before heading home—just the two of us or sometimes a couple of other people as well—every few weeks, but we didn't *know* each other in any real sense.

I had been somewhat distracted at work. No one had really seemed to notice—nobody said anything, anyway.

Now, foolishly, I'd put myself one-on-one with someone, the primary focus of their attention—the only distractions the background scenery of women, and sports on the TV over the bar.

That I was ill at ease, oddly jumpy, was immediately obvious, and something that I had no credible way to explain.

Just trying to *think* of something to say—just a little minor lie to brush the question aside—escalated quickly in my head toward crisis.

What could I tell him?

*I was upset because of something at home?*

*Sick pet or relative?*

*Money worries?*

*Problems with my wife?*

That last one, in particular, almost made me choke on my beer.

What an incredibly dangerous—and *stupid*—conversational door that last one would have been to open.

And, somewhere in the recesses of my brain, I had a niggling anxiety that she would somehow *know* that I had been "over-sharing" or engaging in—never really thought about it this way—disrespectful chatter.

I didn't want to *get-in-trouble.*

Best I could muster was a *cares of the world* sigh and a shrug.

"Ah, you know . . . *stuff.*"

"*Tell-me-about-it,*" Jimmy muttered reflexively, an obligatory gesture of sympathy, flagging down the waitress to get us another beer.

The second problem was peeing.

36

The chastity device had a little slit at the tip, but it was almost impossible to pee *straight*. Maneuvering to line up with the slit was difficult; with my cock all scrunched up, there was no way to aim.

I had quickly learned that I would have to pee sitting down, having sprayed the toilet and the floor the first time I had tried it standing up with the device on.

She had stood there in the doorway to the bathroom, shaking her head in gentle disapproval.

"You get a mop and some cleaning spray," she'd said firmly. "Clean up your mess. Then we'll have to get you changed and—" she couldn't seem to stop a grin from breaking through, "—Mommy will have to teach you how to go potty again."

Sitting down.

And prepared.

Because the process was imperfect at best and required cleaning up. At home I had learned that I could wash myself in the shower or the sink, with the device on, and dry myself—*oh so carefully*—with the hair dryer.

I had felt a burst of gratitude when she prepped me for work, by saying that I would have to remember to always bring paper towels with me into the stall.

*How did she know that?*

"And you want to make sure no one sees you pee, don't you? That's *private*," she'd added, petting my groin. "You be my good boy."

If Jimmy hadn't noticed that anything of consequence was bothering me, he was just as unfazed by my shooting up from my chair and rummaging frantically for my wallet.

*Can't pee?*

*Can't stay.*

"Curfew?" he smiled at me.

A little shard of panic shot through me but then faded: almost everyone at work used that shorthand for getting home to their spouse.

Didn't mean anything.

*To him,* anyway.

I just nodded sheepishly.

"Yeah. Jeez. . . forgot. . ."

Jimmy just gave me a little four-fingered kiddie-wave goodbye and turned his attention back to his beer, the TV, and the waitresses.

Which brings me to the last—and *worst*—thing I did wrong.

*I was late.*

When I hustled up the front walk, she was standing in the doorway, looking through the storm door. She had her fluffy, white, terrycloth bathrobe on and, as I got closer and she opened the door to usher me in, I could see that she held a belt at her side, looped.

"Get in here, young man!" she said curtly, closing both doors.

"Do you have *any* idea how worried I've been?" she demanded, looking me full in the face. "You *know* that you are not allowed to be out alone after dark."

*Did I* "know" that?

"And you are *never* allowed to just change your plans, *willy-nilly,* without asking Mommy's permission. Do you understand me?"

"Yes . . . yes, Mistress Mommy."

I couldn't keep my eyes from flitting constantly to the belt she was holding.

"*I'm up here!*" she snapped redirecting me, making me look into her eyes.

"This is *not* acceptable," she said, rapidly unsnapping and unzipping my pants, shucking them, along with my underwear, down to my knees.

Pointing to the living room, she directed me to one of the corners.

"You go stand there for a while; think about what you've done."

I found a wave of relief, as I shuffled awkwardly to comply, in the fact that the living room curtains were drawn.

But the belt really terrified me.

After that fast initiating experience—when she had awakened me in the middle of the night dressed as if for work, formal and formidable—she had taken to wearing that specific bathrobe around the house. On rare occasions, she would be nude underneath; more often, she wore those large, white, full-cut cotton panties that reached almost to her navel.

No more sexy lingerie around the house.

But, of course, there was something furiously, and disturbingly, exciting about that.

And—how could this *possibly* be?—was there something about the cut of the robe or the way in which she wore it that made it momentarily gape or sway open, when she was walking, when she was sitting, when she was standing, when she was lying in bed?

I was in a near-constant state of erotic jitter, trying to see a flash of her cleavage, her breasts, her legs, her ass, those huge, plain, white, cotton panties.

On Sunday, she had leaned over to get something from a shelf on the refrigerator door; I had seen one of her nipples.

I had a fast rush of excitement at that.

Then she looked up at me quickly, gathering the robe tightly around her neck and said, as if in shock and outrage, "are you *peeking* at Mommy? Are you trying to look under Mommy's robe?"

"I—" in a hot flush of shame, I knew that I had to confess—and did so as rapidly as possible.

She nodded, pursed her lips, made as if to say something then seemed to reconsider.

"I appreciate that you told me the truth," she said softly. "But only *very-bad-little-boys* peek at girls, *especially* their Mommies. If you are supposed to see something, Mommy will show you. If you're not, then you need to not be naughty like that."

"Yes, Mistress Mommy," I murmured.

After the rush of excitement, a flash of shame, I felt a warm wave of relief at the fact that it didn't seem like she was going to punish me.

*Chemicals,* I thought in wonder; it was as if I were an orchestra and she the conductor.

And her clothing had been deftly re-arranged, both reinforcing her authority and making her alluring to me in a series of ways that tangled and confused me.

I didn't really want to think it all through; it was too daunting.

She had been *business sexy* that first night, a little glossy, brisk, and stern. You would notice her at the office—smoky stockings, high heels, skirt a little tight, blouse a little filmy—but she didn't look trashy or fetishistic.

But, from then on, at home, she had become—on the surface at least—almost the *antithesis* of sexy, a study in white cotton concealment: those big panties; that voluminous bathrobe; long, plain, white, sheath nightgowns that fell below her knees, no meaningful cleavage visible at the top.

Which was all *agonizingly* exciting, my heart skipping a beat when she reached up for something and I saw a fast flash of the crescent of soft skin at the edge of her armpit.

*Why?*

And then the fact that I was being turned on by—that I was beginning to *obsess* over—these little innocuous flashes of skin: *it was embarrassing.*

I was furtively trying to see—to *peek*—under these irreproachably chaste garments; I was ashamed by this—and confused.

Except, of course, *I knew.*

I knew *exactly* what it was.

And *she* knew.

And she fed and nurtured my feelings.

Could it have been only once?

Because, almost always, it was gentle chastisement—it could certainly not have been more than twice.

Instead of being stern or softly chiding me, she gave me what looked like a sly, shy, quick smile, leaned in, her hair just grazing my cheek, spoke softly and hotly into my ear, her voice a teasing sing-song, as if we were sharing a naughty secret, something that pleased and flattered her, though she knew it was wrong, and whispered urgently:

"You were peeking at *Mommy! Weren't* you?"

Then a quick nuzzling of my cheek, her nose wiggling playfully in my ear. "I know it's so, *so* hard," she breathed. "But you *try* to be a good boy."

I must have been standing in the corner for fifteen minutes, fretting about the belt, ominous on the couch, wondering if this was the time to put a stop to the whole thing, before she came back.

*Stop.*

*Or Go.*

No middle ground.

She came back in and sat on the couch. I heard the soft jingle of the belt buckle.

"Turn around," she said. "Come stand in front of me."

The robe was loose on top. Standing, it was hard not to look down at her breasts. At the bottom, the robe was parted so that one of her legs was almost fully exposed. I thought I might have seen a flash of her panties, but struggled not to look, to notice, to think.

"Are you trying to peek at Mommy again, young man?" she said sternly.

"No, Mistress Mommy," I said quickly.

"Do you know why Mommy is so angry?" she asked.

I felt like my nose was beginning to run.

Was I tearing up? I *really* had to pee badly.

"Because I was out late and didn't tell you—didn't ask permission?" I said in a rush.

The belt lay on the couch next to her and I fought not to look at it, just as I was trying desperately not to look at her breasts, her legs, her panties.

"That's right," she said. "Mommy was *very* worried. It was dark out and I didn't know where my little boy was. I was getting scared I might have to call the police."

"I'm sorry Mistress Mommy," I managed, trying to keep my voice from breaking. "I really, *really,* have to pee!"

"Mommy knows how beer works," she said with a tight smile.

Finally, I couldn't help looking directly at the belt and sobbing out the question, "Are you going to hit me with the belt?"

She paused—the length of three of my shuddering breaths—looking directly at me with an expression that I couldn't quite read.

She didn't seem to be thinking.

"No," she said finally, her expression softening. "Kneel down for Mommy."

It was awkward with my pants as they were; it was painful with my bladder so full.

She reached out and stroked the side of my face, my hair, my forehead.

"You know that Mommy loves you very much," she said quietly. "Mommy will *always* love you. Even though sometimes you make her angry or make her scared." She reached over to the belt at her side, placed her hand over the buckle. "Mommy doesn't ever *want* to use the belt," she said, pausing, making sure the threat was perfectly clear.

"But you have to be a *good* little boy. You have to be obedient, you have to be polite, you have to not do the nasty things that *bad* boys do."

She hesitated.

"I *know*," she said slowly, "you *think* all kinds of bad things. *All* kinds of bad. *Nasty*. Strange. Disgusting. *Embarrassing*. Scary. *Sick things*. Don't you?"

I was crying; I nodded abjectly.

"You don't have to be ashamed about that," she whispered, still stroking my face. "You have to *be a good* boy—and you have to listen to Mommy—but you can *think* anything you want."

"*Anything*," she said, after another pause and with some force. "It's okay. Mommy really needs you to understand that."

"I love you, too . . . I'm sorry I was bad, Mistress Mommy," I sobbed. "I didn't mean to make you worry. I won't do it again."

"There we go," she crooned. "*That* wasn't so hard, was it? Now we can kiss and make up."

I brought my face to hers, but she turned her head a little.

"Not on Mommy's lips," she said.

I stayed in contact with her cheek for a few moments, not wanting to move.

"Now," she leaned back slightly, parting the top of her robe just a little, but holding it against her skin. I could see more of her cleavage and her breasts, but not the nipples. "You may kiss Mommy here."

It was even harder for me not to linger there, but I felt like I was on the verge of actually wetting myself.

"Now," she said, her voice getting huskier. She parted the bottom of her robe, fully exposing both of her legs, the entirety of the white panties. "You may kiss Mommy on that *big* wet spot," she whispered.

"Just a quick kiss, no tongue, no lingering. Oh *gooooood boy*," she said.

As I obeyed, she first pressed my face tightly up against that damp and fragrant patch of cloth, rubbing the evidence of her arousal on my nose and my cheeks, then pushed me gently back, with what seemed like some regret.

"Go on now," she said, a little breathlessly. "You scoot to the potty. We don't want any accidents," calling after me as I quickly complied, almost tripping on my pants, "you wash your hands nice and clean, and brush your teeth, but you do *not* have Mommy's permission to wash your face."

The relief of peeing was just incredible. It wasn't an orgasm but it was damn close.

From down the hall, in our bedroom, came a ferocious pulse of wailing and then the intense keening sound of *her* orgasm, which seemed to go on forever, almost drowning out the steady buzz of her vibrator.

## Chapter Six: Helping Mommy

It was a week before she took the chastity device off for the first time.

I went down on her every night, licking and sucking her to one or two orgasms, continuing, per instruction, to gently lap at her softly until she fell asleep.

Most mornings, as soon as she woke up, she would drowsily instruct me to "be a good boy and bring Mommy her alarm clock," that powerful wand vibrator that perked her up more reliably than a cup of coffee.

"Mommies need *lots* of cummies!" she would tell me. "And you're a *good* boy for helping Mommy. Boys who have too many cummies aren't healthy," she said gravely. "It makes them mean and selfish and they don't clean up their messes. You don't want to be one of those bad, selfish, boys who does those nasty things do you?" she'd ask, shaking her head from side to side in a way that clearly meant I should follow suit.

In our previous reality, I had masturbated daily; she had seemed to enjoy orgasms like a weekly night out at a decent but not spectacular restaurant. The *diet* she had put me on was radical; the hunger *she* now displayed was hard for me to fathom.

"No, Mistress Mommy," I would say, a little glumly.

After three days, my balls started to ache; after five I began to leak pre-cum.

On Friday night, I had just started to trace the smooth swollen folds of her cunny with my tongue, the chastity cage like a ring of barbed wire, when she gently pushed my head away.

She made a humming, rising and falling sound, as if she were thinking.

"Have you seen Mommy's new *dildie?*" she asked, her tone almost shy.

"No, Mistress Mommy."

"You have permission to look in Mommy's special drawer and take out Mommy's new *dildie* for her!"

She said this like it was a special treat for me.

Reluctantly, I went to her night table and opened the drawer.

The new dildo was on top of a small pile of other sex toys, some of them familiar to me, some of them not; I didn't dare spend any extra time trying to figure out what was what.

It was tan; longer and thicker than my cock; heavily laced with veins; ribs and what looked like some kind of clitoral stimulator near the base; another set of raised ridges on the top side that I assumed to be for G-Spot stimulation.

When I lifted it up, it felt heavy.

"Mistress Mommy," I whispered, without turning to face her. "Can I *please* be your *dildie* tonight . . . *please?*"

"Awwww . . . does your wee-wee really hurt?" she asked.

I nodded.

"Turn around and face Mommy," she said, her voice a little thick.

46

I turned.

She was lying partially on her side, one arm above her on the pillow the other disappearing under her body, legs parted just enough so that her finger tips were intermittently visible as they lazily traced and explored that slickly lubricated crease, making an only faintly audible clicking sound in the syrup of her arousal.

"Ask Mommy again," she breathed. "Ask Mommy *properly* . . . mmmmm—like a *good* boy."

"Please Mistress Mommy," I managed. "My wee-wee *really* hurts."

She gave a little grunt, prompting more.

"Please Mistress Mommy . . . can I . . . can I *please* be your *dildie?*"

For a few moments, the only sound was the accelerating dance of those wet fingertips. Then that music slowed and finally stopped and she sighed, as if in regret.

"Okay," she said softly, "get Mommy her bathrobe and we'll get your wee-wee ready. But this is a very special occasion," she cautioned. "This is *not* going to become a regular thing."

"Yes Mistress Mommy," I said meekly.

She took the robe, put it on, and I followed her into the bathroom. I wasn't allowed to wear pajamas, so there was nothing for me to remove.

I had always slept nude; that was my preference, it was how I had been most comfortable.

But when she *forbade* me clothing in bed, "Mommy needs to *always* be able to see that your wee-wee is properly secured and that you are *not* playing with it without permission," she sexualized what had always been unremarkable to me.

Appearing to think for a moment, she directed me to stand in the bathtub. She reached into her bathrobe pocket and took out the key, snapped open the padlock that held the device shut and put it on the edge of the sink.

I was half-hard—about as hard as I could get, confined as I was—and that and my pubic hair made it difficult to pull the device off.

She reached for the container of liquid soap on the sink, squirted some onto her hands, then gently traced it around the edges where the device was stuck.

"We're going to have to get rid of all this nasty *hair*," she murmured to me. "It's *hurting* you!" she added almost with indignation, the hair something for which she had no further tolerance.

The device slipped fully off and my cock immediately and painfully swelled to full size.

A clear drop of pre-cum popped out and ran down the shaft.

"*Awww,*" she said as if in sympathy, "it's *crying*. It *really* must *hurt*."

"Poor little wee-wee," she said, tracing the little wet trail, looking for a moment like she was going to lick her finger but then bringing it instead up to my mouth, for me to lick and suck clean, feeding me a mixture of soap and my own pre-cum.

"Good boy," she said. "Now let's take care of all that nasty hair."

I was surprised by how efficiently she shaved me, lathering me up with feathery touches, pulling my scrotum deftly from side to side, holding skin here and there taut, smoothly gliding the triple-edged razor around my cock.

Still, I was lightheaded with the combination of fear that I would be cut and the anticipation of what was to come.

She left not a single nick.

Then she took a facecloth and ran it through hot water in the sink, squeezed it out, and expertly swabbed off all the stray jots of shaving cream.

"There we *go*," she breathed in approval of her own work. "Now all we have to do is make sure that you're nice and *clean*."

She ran the hot water again, until there was a little steam, passed the cloth through, squeezed it out, wrapped it around my entire hard cock.

Squeezing tightly, she pulled it from base to head, pausing there as though polishing a doorknob, twisting the towel roughly and thoroughly.

*"Oww, Mommy . . . !"* I started.

But she was done, and just looked at me neutrally, as though I were behaving inexplicably.

"It's important," she said, "that your wee-wee be *very* clean. You understand that, don't you?"

I said that I did.

"Okay then, let's go back to Mommy's bed!" like a fun adventure.

She kept the robe on, but fully open, lying down on her back, propping her head up slightly with an extra pillow, as though she were preparing to watch.

"Get between Mommy's legs," she urged me.

I did, holding myself up on my arms and my knees. My cock was still fully, painfully, *unimaginably,* hard— throbbing, pre-cum leaking in a steady stream now; it was hot, red, and exquisitely sensitized from the scrubbing she'd given it.

I was beginning to feel an inkling of worry, but I was almost in a panic to fuck her at that point, I couldn't—I didn't want to—think about anything else.

She traced the wet and swollen lips of her cunt with two fingers, the fingers of the other hand just barely surrounding and brushing the head of my cock.

"You're *sure* you want to be Mommy's *dildie,"* she said hoarsely, "you're *sure* you can do this?"

"Yes Mommy . . . oh please, *please* Mommy!"

She placed the head of my cock just at the hot slick entrance to her cunt; I pushed a glorious inch inside—just the ridge of the crown through her tighter inner lips.

She gasped, then grunted, and it felt like she had tightened a pulsing rubber band around the excruciatingly sensitive head of my cock—something she had *never* done before; where could she have learned to *do* that? was that the result of Kegel exercises?—triggering, almost *sucking* out of me, an instant *torrent,* a saved-up week's-worth, of cum.

I gave a wail of frustration and defeat.

"Oh *poor-little-boy!"* she cried. "Oh, your poor wee-wee!"

"I'm sorry Mistress Mommy, I'm *so* sorry. . .!"

"I *know,"* she said gently. "I know you tried. It's okay, there are some things that little boys just aren't good at. But there are other ways you can help Mommy."

I nodded miserably against her shoulder, not wanting to raise my head, to look at her, to do anything.

She took a moment to bring her own breathing back under control; she hadn't cum but she had clearly felt a surge of *something* that almost shimmered off her body.

She let me rest quietly, stroking my hair, nuzzling my ear a little, making little shushing noises.

"Okay," she said, after a few minutes.

She didn't say it explicitly, but it was clear that I was to get up.

I did.

She remained on her back, legs slightly open.

"Come sit up here," she said, patting the head of the bed. "What did we learn?" she asked, sounding quite serious.

"Mommy . . . ?"

"Well, you wanted to help—and that's good—like you help Mommy fall asleep and you help with Mommy's alarm clock in the morning. You wanted to help by being

50

Mommy's *dildie* and . . . well," she looked down at the pool of cum on her belly and between her legs, on the bathrobe beneath her, which had at least spared the sheet, then back at me.

"Your wee-wee made a *very* big mess," she said softly. "And it didn't even really get very far into Mommy's cunny, did it? Hardly at all?" she said in a tone of sympathetic surprise, tinged with disappointment.

I shook my head miserably.

"So what have we learned?" she asked again.

"The *dildie* is better than me," I muttered a little sullenly.

"Why?" she said, not taking issue with my tone or volume but demanding more.

"It's bigger," I offered.

"And?" she prompted.

"It's always hard for Mommy . . . ?"

"That's right," she said. "*Good!* What else?"

"It never cums too fast," I whispered.

"*Very* good!" she said, pulling my head toward her and giving me a loud, sexless kiss on the cheek.

"So, this is okay," she said softly. "*It's okay.* It didn't work out the way you hoped it would, but you've learned something, *that's* what's important."

I found the lesson—and her enthusiasm for it—a little chilling, but she was being so warm and so kind, forgiving me . . . for a disaster that *she* had meticulously engineered?

But I stopped on the precipice of *it's not fair!* and *it wasn't my fault!* unable, and too ashamed, to argue with Mommy.

And was there some emotional charge I got from that shame—or from the ritual of apology and absolution?

Was there some odd way in which the feeling that she was steadily withdrawing some of the privileges of her body that I had long taken for granted—was that a *relief?*

51

I took a deep breath and let it float away.

"Okay," she said sternly. "Now. You *still* have to clean up the mess you made with your wee-wee, just like you would have had to if you had been more . . . *successful.*"

I hung my head, nodded silently in resignation.

"Then we'll get your bowl of ice and your towel and make you all nice and secure again!"

## Chapter Seven: Hints

There were the things she did.

There were the things she said.

There were the things she promised.

Together they were a powerful drug: hypnotic, stimulating, aphrodisiac.

But there was a gossamer web woven around those realities—of implications, hints, *not-quite-threats*—that was more powerful still, that kept me in a constant state of childlike awe and excitement, stunned at what was happening, anxiously anticipating what might come next; there was always a slight tinge of fear, spicing my jittery, *rarely-to-be-satisfied*, desire.

She called me into her room one evening, had me lie on the bed on my belly; finding a position that didn't hurt my confined cock and swollen balls was difficult.

"Close your eyes," she said softly, kneeling on the mattress next to me.

She began tracing her fingertips lightly back and forth, up and down my body, from the nape of my neck to my feet—which made me flinch in surprise at her first light touch.

She paused for a moment to shush me gently, then continued, humming a little atonally under her breath, as if in thought.

She lightly stroked the juncture of my shoulder and my neck; I could feel her hair brush my back as she leaned in to do this. Her fingers went slowly side to side at the small of my back, a metronome, a single finger pausing for just a moment at the very top of the cleft of my buttocks— a jolt I tried to suppress.

I felt her move down the bed slightly, then trace both of my calves at the same time, just the sides of my feet, then up to the backs of my knees, linger for a quick second higher up, on my inner thighs.

The mattress shifted with her weight as she straddled me just below my ass, my legs between hers, her bathrobe still on. There were further adjustments and then she lay flat on top of me, robe open at the top and bottom, but still firmly cinched, the knot in the small of my back, my swollen cock and balls compressed even more painfully.

Her nipples were hard against my shoulder blades, her *mons*, almost always shaved completely smooth, meticulously moisturized, soft and pampered, an unexpectedly raspy patch of stubble—again, just at the top of the cleft of my ass.

She sighed, lay her cheek on my back, her nose just at my shoulder, pulled my arms to full upward extension at an angle, paralleled them with her own.

The furious excitement of her contact with my body, the multiple sensations, the smell of her hair, the feel and the sound of her breathing almost in my ear, the ceaseless throbbing pain of my imprisoned cock and balls, trepidation, gratitude, feverish desire: my sense of time was entirely vaporized.

She might have fallen asleep; I might have gone into a trance.

But I could hear her continued humming to herself—sometimes hard to distinguish from her breathing—and very slowly became aware of a miniscule, intermittent circle of scratchy pressure as she began, almost absentmindedly, to rub against me with that little patch of pubic stubble.

For a moment I stopped breathing; my mind raced; I tried to think of absolutely nothing.

Gradually, the pressure and the motion increased, her humming becoming a little louder, sounding somehow thoughtful.

After a period of time that I could not possibly calculate, she sighed, moved her hands in close to my body as if doing pushups, lifted her legs and brought them together on top of and between mine.

I felt the scrape of her toenails against my calves; her knees pushed my legs apart; she made a murmur of satisfaction as she settled between my thighs, her raspy *mons* carefully back in place, in that cleft, now slightly spread.

Bringing her arms in tight and folding them almost underneath herself, hands open but flexed, she rested her fingernails on either side of my neck, as though preparing to play the piano. Her head was up now, her mouth right behind my ear. The hard pebbles of her nipples came back into contact with my shoulder blades.

There was another seemingly endless pause.

Then she began pressing against me again, first those slow circles, then something more like thrusting.

In my ear, the humming was deeper, slightly louder, an engine moving deliberately from idle to low rev.

She had said not a word.

I could not prevent myself from opening my eyes for just a flash; I had my cheek against the mattress, my head pointed in the direction of her night table, which housed *Mommy's Special Drawer.*

She saw me peek and gave a two-grunt admonition and warning—*mm, mm!*—in sync with quick, raspy twitches against me.

Maintaining the same slow rhythm, she increased the pressure—eliciting an occasional squeak when I was compressed from a particularly painful angle—her motion becoming a slight downward slide, followed by a forward and upward thrust, her fingernails pulsing in time, indenting but not breaking my skin.

I could feel the lips of her cunt swell, the sting of her sweat on my abraded skin; the stubble, still sharp, slick with her lubrication, which I could hear as well as feel. The humming had turned into a deeper, more intense— though not that much louder—series of grunts, in cadence with her thrusting: a sound of effort and determination, satisfaction and perhaps some anger.

My squeaking, and involuntary expulsion of breath, became regular punctuation. I might have been able to cum, even with the chastity cage on, but the pulsing pain made it impossible. Her fingernails started to regularly slip off my shoulders and scratch a short distance down my back. The salty sting of our combined sweat suggested what I would confirm the following morning, that she had broken the skin.

I could feel her thighs clench together and begin to tremble, as she increased her tempo and pressure.

When she came, with three final—louder, deeper, longer—grunts of effort, she went more or less slack on top of me. She spread her legs, and mine with them, dropped her head back onto my shoulders, sweaty strands of her hair plastered against the rows of scratches. Her breasts felt softer against me as a series of spasms, jerks, and tremors coursed through her body, peaked, ebbed, and trickled to a stop.

After a few moments, she sighed, rolled off me, kissed the nape of my neck.

She curled up on her side with her back to me.

Flopping an arm behind herself, flailing softly to find me, she gave me a gentle shove.

"Okay!" she said, in what sounded like an attempt at a bright voice that was overtaken by a tired, post-orgasmic slur, "You can go to *your* bed now!" and seemed to fall instantly asleep.

I now had my own room.

I went there in a daze but sleep was a long time coming.

The throb of that unrelieved pressure—now even *more* intense—would not let up.

And whenever I thought I had calmed down enough to drift off, my heart would begin hammering again, my breathing becoming ragged, my head clanging both with the excitement of what had happened and the slightly pleasurable fear of what might come next.

Should I take what she had done this evening as a hint?

I wondered.

# Part III:  Letting Go

## Chapter Eight: Fridays

Friday became the day for my "weekly cummy."

But if—*ever* so briefly—that was something that I looked forward to with anticipation, it almost immediately became clear that it was a day designed to *teach me lessons,* to combine frustration with what little relief I got.

After a few days of letting my pubic stubble grow—a steadily increasing, constant, maddening itch—she established a rhythm of shaving me every other day, usually at bed time.

"Be a good boy," she'd cue me, softly but firmly. "Go get your ice and your towel."

I would obey her and go to the bathroom to wait.

Sometimes she followed almost immediately on my heels; sometimes she made me wait. The combination of consistent ritual and inconsistent timing kept me on edge.

That brief period of itchy stubble had quickly taught me that her shaving me regularly was important, something I should *want* and *welcome.*

And if that absence of hair was somewhat emasculating—why did the removal of *her* pubic hair have exactly the *opposite* effect, *increasing* her power and her femininity?—I quickly came to secretly enjoy that smoothness.

Of course she encouraged me in that direction.

And—when I thought about it, really—the diametrically opposite effects made sense.

For a woman, absent that curtain of obscuring hair— shaved bare—there's a boldness, a brazen statement to men, taunting and powerful:

*Go on,* try *not to look.*

And, of course, fail.

*Try not to think about what you so* desperately *want to do to it—remember the childhood yearning you could not yet quite name, the unquenchable adolescent flame of a desire ever-present, but almost always frustrated.*

And fail.

*Try not to think about the things—*entirely *beyond limit—that* it *can make you do.*

And shiver.

For men, it lays bare an area where we can be most badly hurt physically—*No hitting below the belt!*—and psychically, turns us back into little boys.

Women don't need to look.

And when they do, there is the humiliation of the inevitable response: *Oh, isn't that* cute!

Nude and denuded, I walked around the house with nervous anticipation hovering always in the background— complemented by that intense frustrated desire and that heightened, almost paralytic, awareness of her power.

That she then covered up what she had exposed— under those large, white, cotton panties; beneath the outer layer of her white terrycloth robe—somehow stoked my desire further yet.

It was dizzyingly erotic when I caught a glimpse under her robe: of the bold outline of the lips of her denuded cunt, when the panties were pulled tight; of the wet spot that often appeared when she teased, taunted, or humbled me.

And when she opened her robe for me, peeled down those panties, exposing herself so that I could service her in whatever way her whims or desires dictated, it was as if she knew that the rationing of my access was an important safeguard, keeping me from being simply too overwhelmed to function.

She would soothe me as I worshipfully followed her instructions—laving, licking, sucking, caressing—as if she knew the primal fear that required calming, murmuring that I was such a good boy, that I should give in to the needs of her cunt, that I should surrender to the needs that it created in me.

"You *can't* resist," she would sigh, sometimes with a tinge of wonder to her voice. "Mommy's cunny's needs are *so* strong. Give in, little boy, give in to your *need* to serve Mommy's cunny."

"That's *all* you need to do; that's all that *matters*; that's all there *is* in the world: your *need*. Can you *feel* it? Can you feel it *pulse* and *throb* through your imprisoned little wee-wee? Can you feel it fluttering in your tummy, thudding in your chest? You *need* to serve Mommy's cunny."

That every-other-day rhythm of her shaving me reinforced the dynamic.

Like clockwork, that faintest hint of stubble, that shadow of the possibility of adulthood, was deftly and completely removed—those few minutes of regular freedom, of her handling me, her touch a blessing and a curse, never enough pressure for me to cum, were blissful, but only increased my frustration, the intensity of my sexual desire.

I came to realize—too late?—that what she was performing was an inside-out coming of age ritual, metronomically pushing me back from the brink of maturity, gently but firmly, a ceremony in which she demonstrated, with almost hypnotic intensity, that both my body and my very *age*, were under her sole and direct power, subservient to the authority she had taken—that I had *given* her—to actually stop time.

It was rare that she would hurt me during this procedure, only occasionally reaching down to first cup, then grip, then squeeze my balls, with an intensity that increased until I couldn't stop myself from making a noise, or my legs began to give—which, it quickly became apparent, was the only signal she would deign to heed.

"Those are *very* swollen," she would say, wide-eyed as if in surprise.

"So many cummies trying to get out! I bet you can't *wait* until Friday."

She took to coating my cock and balls with baby oil before locking me back up. This made for less chafing—and for oily underwear—day-to-day, but the process itself almost drove me out of my mind.

Sometimes we needed a second bowl of ice before my cock would get soft enough to be "secured" again.

The Friday after she had engineered my mortifying failure to fuck her, she had shaved me quickly and was gently oiling me. She hadn't yet said how I was to have my cummy.

I was afraid to ask her, but I was desperate.

In the beginning my cock had throbbed in its deprivation and denial; then my balls began to ache; finally, I reached the point where they treated me instead to, unpredictably intermittent, sharp stabs of pain, throughout the day—sometimes waking me up at night.

Trembling, I whispered, "Mistress Mommy, can you *please* kiss my wee-wee?"

I was standing in the tub and she was sitting on the edge, her head roughly level with my bobbing, now glistening, cock.

She looked up at me for a few moments, seeming to consider this.

"Well. . ." she finally said. "Just *one* kiss. I guess that would be okay. You *have* been a good boy this week."

*One?!*

"Mistress Mommy *wait* . . . !" I started, panicked that she was going to use this to deprive me of what was supposed to be my weekly relief.

But she didn't seem to hear me, quickly closing the paltry distance and engulfing the head of my cock, just bringing the ridge of the crown between her teeth, which she lightly pulsed, sucking furiously, assaulting me at the same time with an unexpected swirling of her tongue, and making a humming sound as she might when deep in thought.

I came *immediately*—and copiously—my legs wobbly, almost falling backward in the tub, my vision blurring a little.

She held fast, keeping me *just* in her mouth, glaring up at me steadily, making little grunts of indignation—real or feigned.

I heard no sounds of swallowing.

She took it all, though she stopped any kind of stimulation as soon as I started cumming—save the menacing vibration of the sounds she was making.

When I had almost stopped shuddering, she pulled back slowly, maintaining the suction, dragging her teeth across the now unbelievably—post-orgasm—sensitive head of my cock.

It remained hard, continuing to leak.

She rose from the edge of the tub until we were face-to-face, her lips pursed, her expression angry.

She took my face firmly in one hand, pincered my cheeks between index finger and thumb, making me gape like a fish, sealed her mouth over mine and forcefully expelled the entire, huge, glob of cum into my mouth, then pulled back and glared at me, as if daring me to do anything other than immediately swallow.

I gagged, coughed, but managed to get it all down.

*"Your wee-wee spat at Mommy!"* she said furiously.

"That's *disgusting!* Mommy tries to show her little boy her love and affection, tries to protect him and take care of him; an innocent kiss and *this* is what happens! You should be *ashamed* of yourself!"

I was speechless and terrified, my mouth gaping open and closing again, lips sticky with my own cum.

She spun away from me, grabbed a bottle of mouthwash off the sink, slurped, rinsed, and spat.

*"This* is why little boys have to have their cummies controlled!" she said angrily. "*This* is why their wee-wees can only be allowed out once in a while!"

I was confused to the point that it felt like my brain was short-circuiting.

Before this had all started—when we were . . . *normal?*—she had swallowed cum.

She'd given me a blow job once a month or so, often during her period. She hadn't appeared to like it very much; she'd pause for a moment after I came, then swallow; I had told her that her spitting instead sort of ruined the afterglow for me.

But it had been almost like a maintenance procedure, the efficient bleeding of a pressure valve.

She had *never* given me a blow job even *remotely* like the one she had just dispensed—albeit with such devastating and deft rapidity: mere seconds to trigger me; a fraction of a minute during which she subtly ruined the orgasm; another moment or two to feed me my own cum.

The *way* she had done it—as she had milked the cum from me the week before when I had just barely penetrated her, demonstrating muscular control (and strength!), and a dexterity she had never before seemed to possess—it was confusing.

I was awed by it.

It was as though she had been a sometime weekend runner who went overnight to running—and *winning!*—marathons.

Of course, *everything* had changed; my entire life—or the home half of it anyway—had been turned upside down. But most of that was by assertion on her part, things that she decided, things that I accepted or things that she simply made me do.

This was different, the steady revelation of—what could one call them but—*skills?*

It was as though she had received training.

It was repellant swallowing cum like that—even worse than usual.

I had accepted this condition at the outset; I had found reading about it, or looking at pornographic images of it, fiercely exciting; she'd known that and used it. But the reality, of course, was far different than what I had imagined.

Had she coached and coaxed me towards this by first having me lick it from her cunt—her belly, her hand—by conditioning me more and more to obey without hesitation or question?

But the instant I thought about how disgusting what she had done to me was, I realized that this was exactly what I had always expected *her* to do. More than that, I had wanted her to do it as if it were at least neutral, if not outright pleasurable for her.

And if what was wrong was being *forced* to consume one's own fluids, I had done that to her too, running my fingers in and out of her cunt and then bringing them to her lips for her to taste; or pressing her hand down to encourage her to stroke herself, then doing the same. Sometimes she had acquiesced, sometimes not; as exciting as I found this, again, she had generally been, at best, neutral.

Snatching the wooden hair brush off the sink, she firmly grabbed my cock, *still* hard, and gave me three fast swats right on the crown.

"Very! *Bad!* Wee-wee!"

I was still oozing and dribbling cum, a streak of which got onto the brush, which seemed to make her more angry still.

*"You clean this right up!"* she said, thrusting it in my face.

I gave it a thorough lick.

I was *still* hard—something she had clearly come to treat as a barometer: if I didn't go soft, I couldn't have been *too* badly hurt; and I must have been taking *some* pleasure in what was being done to me.

I was in awe of her anger as well.

It didn't seem feigned or in any way put on; it seemed genuine.

But—over the many years that we had known each other—I had *never* seen her in a state anything like this. *What did that mean?*

If I was finding some peace in acceptance—giving in, being directed, being punished, being relieved of responsibility, some core set of needs that had been repressed or ignored or long unsatisfied—what previously untapped well of needs, desires, feelings, was *she* now freely allowing to geyser out?

If my biggest preoccupation for the weeks we had been in these new roles had been an ongoing and growing confusion about who *I* was—whether I had ever really known myself; whether I had ever really let anyone *else* know me—pulled into sharp focus now was the question of who *she* was, and if I had ever really known *her.*

It was disturbing.

But it was exciting as well; the barometer doesn't lie.

Was part of what was happening an analog to early or midlife divorcing and remarrying, growing tired of, or just too routinized and comfortable with, a mate and finding a new one—but doing it instead by radically changing the relationship we were in, rather than finding a new one?

It took *two* bowls of ice to calm and shrink me down sufficiently, so that I could be secured again.

I apologized profusely, a constant, babbling stream; she snapped at me in response; there was no forgiveness on offer.

At one point, when the second bowl of ice wasn't enough to immediately shrink me down, she furiously ordered me to turn around, bend over, and put my hands on my knees.

She quickly and roughly pushed an ice cube into my ass; I started and only barely restrained myself from jumping away from her.

"Oww! *Mommy, why . . . ?*" I blubbered, bursting into tears.

"You know *exactly* why!" she snapped. "Maybe *that* will cool off my bad, *bad,* little boy. And his disgusting. Rude. *Inconsiderate,* little, wee-wee!"

Yes.

I knew exactly why.

She made me sleep on the floor at the foot of her bed, giving me a blanket but refusing me a sheet or a pillow.

It was a long, uncomfortable, night.

In the morning, it seemed at first as if the storm had passed.

*"Lit-tle bo-oy,"* she crooned lyrically, waking me from what felt like only moments of rest, "you be a good little boy and bring Mommy her alarm clock."

I scampered to get her the vibrator and, as she took it, she patted the bed next to her.

"You can be in Mommy's bed this morning while Mommy . . . *wakes up.*"

She put my head on her chest, holding it there with one hand, manipulating the vibrator with the other.

It was as if the previous night's rage had unleashed some further, *primal,* power within her—the sounds she made deeper and louder grunts and groans than I had heard before, bestial, *angry* sounds.

She quickly came twice, then pushed me off and flipped onto her belly, the vibrator under her, still buzzing.

"Get between Mommy's legs," she growled at me, spreading them slightly, "and you lick Mommy's asshole while she wakes up! You lick it very, *very*, thoroughly!"

She came at least twice more, while I did as she told me, the inarticulate sounds getting louder and louder, the crests punctuated by the same words, which were not *Mommy-like* at all.

"Uhhhhn . . . ! *Yes!* Yes! *Fuck*, yes! *Fuck*, yes! *Fuck* yes!"

When she had switched off the vibrator, it took her some time to stop shaking. She didn't tell me to stop, so I didn't; she seemed to find it soothing.

Finally, she reached back and pushed my head away—a little roughly.

"Go to the bathroom and wash your hands and face and rinse out your mouth," she said. "Then come back to Mommy."

When I returned, she was sitting up in bed, her back against the headboard. She patted the space for me, then put my head in her lap and randomly tousled my hair.

The smell of her wet cunt—almost touching my nose—was overwhelmingly exciting; it made me lightheaded.

Playing with my hair for a while seemed to calm her down.

"Mommy got *very* angry last night, didn't she?" she mused after some time, almost back to the warmer tone that she usually used, a little dreamily—as if she were talking about someone else, a distant place or time, a slight edge of wonder in her voice—but still with some steel to it.

"Yes, Mistress Mommy," I whispered to her belly.

"And that was *very* silly of Mommy to put something in your bottom—and to make you lick Mommy's bottom!" that last part in the tone she would use to say "*Wasn't that a* strange *movie!*"

"Yes, Mistress Mommy," I whispered again.

"And you still remember why Mommy got mad?" she asked, a little rising inflection, a review quiz.

"Yes, Mistress Mommy . . . I . . . my wee-wee. . . *spat* at you.   And that was . . . it was very rude and inconsiderate . . . and I'll *never* do that again—and, and I'm *very* sorry."

"You'll *never* do that again," she repeated thoughtfully.

"Okay," she leaned down and kissed me tenderly on the forehead, "Mommy forgives you. It's okay now. You did some bad things, some shameful, *disgusting* things. But you apologized—and made promises about future behavior—like a good boy, like the good boy that you are."

## Chapter Nine:  Fault Lines

There were—I wasn't sure how to think about them, spikes or jolts or sudden flashes of insight and change, like the unprecedented storm of her rage—rare instances when I actually *saw* something shift.

You *feel* earthquakes or—more often—little seismic tremors.

A couple of times, it was as if I was there at the moment when the rocky ground underfoot suddenly fissured, a canyon forming before my very eyes, an awesome, terrifying, but somehow beautiful, sight, nature radically remaking the landscape.

I lay naked, on my side, curled toward her on the bed, one evening; she was on her back, robe unbelted, legs and the full expanse of her white cotton panties exposed, most of her abdomen and a wide valley of cleavage uncovered, but the top drawn a little closer together, breasts partly obscured, nipples not quite visible.

She had one hand resting on her belly, fingers splayed.

With the other, she was petting the chastity cage that constricted my cock, her rhythm steady but slow and light, the way you might stroke a puppy's head.

"I know your wee-wee is very scrunched up in there," she sighed, and I nodded against her shoulder.

"I know it hurts."

I nodded again.

"It hurts?" she prompted. "*Tell Mommy.*"

Her hand went lower on her belly, her fingertips moving slowly, side to side, just grazing the elastic at the top of her panties.

"My wee-wee hurts," I whispered, "the way it's all scrunched up."

She made a thoughtful noise, her hand pausing, the tip of her middle finger just beginning to indent the flesh above the waistband.

"And because Mommy has taken control of your pleasure," she said softly. "Isn't that right?"

"Mommy controls my pleasure," I whispered.

"And you've been *very* good," she said, sounding sincere—admiring, impressed—her fingers moving again for a moment along the band, her hand then sliding down over the panties, the heel of her palm pressing in just a little, describing a small, slow, lazy circle.

"Mommy sees how hard you're working on your training. Mommy," she paused for a breath, "*sees.*"

For a moment, the only sounds in the world came from her breathing: slow, steady, the almost imperceptible sound of her palm against the fabric; I strained for the tiny clicking notes of the lubricated folds she only rarely allowed me to see unless I was servicing her—sometimes, even then, she would blindfold me—my nostrils flaring, trying to catch a whiff of her arousal.

"And sometimes Mommy *teases* you," she said finally, thoughtful, even a little morose. "Sometimes, even when you're trying *so* hard to be good, and Mommy *doesn't even have a reason*, she's still *very* mean to you, very *cruel* to your poor. *Trapped.* Wee-wee."

In what space it had, my cock immediately bulged furiously against its restraint; there was a surge of pain in my swollen balls. She stopped petting me; the stroking against her panties pausing, as well.

"Oh!" she cried softly, at least partly in surprise. "Your wee-wee just *jumped,* when Mommy talked about being mean, didn't it?"

I gulped but said nothing.

*"Didn't it?"* she said again, this time with a bit of a nasty edge, giving my balls a quick squeeze, firm but not too hard.

"Yes, Mommy," I whispered miserably.

She ran her fingers over my upper arm.

"And it's making you *shiver,* too!" she whispered in discovery. "It's giving you *goosebumps!*"

Her hand returned to the edge of the elastic, hesitated for just a moment and then disappeared up to her wrist under that bright white expanse of cotton.

"And it," she paused to breathe again, this time neither as slowly nor as evenly as before, "it makes Mommy's clitty just *burn,*" she said, her fingers moving slowly, slightly stretching and tenting the fabric, as though she were a hesitant and cautious typist, "it *burns* when Mommy's mean to your wee-wee, when she knows that it's leaking *tears* of agonizing, frustrated desire, that you're just getting *feverish,*" the speed of her typing picked up a little, "feverish with your desperate *need* for what Mommy won't, won't*, won't* let you have."

When she got stuck on that word, she tossed her head back and forth, eyes closed; her legs began to move almost imperceptibly, as though she were asleep, swimming in her dreams across a lake of warm honey, her stroke microscopically precise, glacially slow.

"And that *pain* in your frustrated, trapped wee-wee," she let out a long moan, "it just *throbs* through Mommy's clitty so, so, *so* beautifully. You need Mommy, you need Mommy, you need Mommy," she muttered the repetition, then grunted, "You *need* Mommy to be mean to you."

I was no longer just shivering, I was shaking.

She was beginning to tremble as well.

*"Don't you!"* she said sharply.

I nodded hurriedly and made soft, mewling affirmative sounds, feeling flushed, slightly sick, aroused with an intensity that made me wonder if I might be having a heart attack.

"You need to help Mommy feed that terrible. *Throbbing.* Pain. Of cruel, cruel, *cruel* denial. To her mean. *Selfish.* Hungry. *Angry.* Throbbing. Clitty."

"And its appetite—*ohhhh!,* the more you *feed* it—it *just.* Keeps," another long moan, and then a hoarse whisper, *"Growing."*

The movement beneath her panties took on a frantic and disorganized pace. She was no longer stroking me; it felt, instead, as if her hand were in the throes of some kind of seizure, flapping about, her fingers spasmodically opening and closing, sometimes over my cock, sometimes not, a lobster blindly flailing, desperate to pincer its prey.

As if by itself, obeying a different regime of gravity or magnetism, her body was beginning to arch off the bed, her shoulders and her heels the points of contact, her torso from neck to knees bowing upward from the middle, as if her pelvis were being drawn toward the ceiling.

She was almost beyond speech, her sounds more those of a weightlifter struggling at the edge of her capabilities, but as the grunting got faster and a little higher in tone, she regained control of her hand, long enough at least to grasp my imprisoned cock at the base, below my balls, lock on tight, and pulse a surreal rainbow of pain through my body—if I screamed, I couldn't hear myself, endorphins flooding my head, my ears sealed as if with warm oil, my vision blurred, perhaps with tears—as I arched toward, rather than away from her, *toward* the torment: my pain and abject surrender, gasoline to the surging fire of her arousal.

Beneath the grunting, I could make out a mutter like a prayer, initially indistinct; but as she moved toward, into, finally through a *terrifying* orgasm, it became first intelligible and then a rhythmic shout—though in a strangled, gravelly tone, a voice much deeper than I had ever heard her use before.

In time to her squeezing of my cock, she was chanting.

"Feed Mommy's clitty. *Feed* Mommy's Clitty! FEED. *Mommy's. CLITTY!*" until the violent, spastic, shuddering arch of her body broke, surrendering once again to gravity—and a seeming lack of oxygen made it impossible for her to resist falling back onto the bed, sheened in sweat, the last tremors trickling unevenly to a stop, her pincering and squeezing trailing off as well, the last thing I remember before I fell into a dazed and exhausted sleep.

I hadn't dared touch her.

I hadn't cum.

I hadn't been stimulated, really, by anything other than pain, her voice, her scent, her *confession*, the horrific spectacle of her pleasure.

It had been a sexual experience that surpassed in intensity almost anything that had ever happened to me before.

We would never talk about it.

But she had come to understand something.

She'd crystalized it, named it for both of us with clarity and precision, spoken truths that neither of us would ever be able to deny, unsheathed claws that—I was sure at the time—could never be retracted.

She could be careful with them—if she so chose—but neither of us would ever be able to forget that they were there.

## Chapter Ten: Mommy's Boyfriend

I could hear the sounds as soon as I stepped through the door.

It took a few moments for me to separate the words from the stream of panting and moaning, but the rhythms alone immediately stopped me in the front hall, my face, my neck, and my upper chest instantly sheened in a cold sweat.

As the words became clear I could hear, as well, a whining, desperate note to her repeated plea, in response to which my cock surged and pulsed painfully against the chastity device.

"*Please!*" the word drawn out from a moan almost to a sob, "Mommy's boyfriend is *too* big . . . It feels like he's going to split her apart! *Please!*"

I let the sounds draw me through the house in a daze, to the doorway of the bedroom, where she was writhing on her back, alone, on top of the comforter, her work clothes in the kind of disarray that suggested an assault: blouse untucked and half open, bra still on but pushed up, exposing her breasts, which bore what looked like red pinch marks; skirt rucked up to her waist, one spike-heeled mule on the floor—beside a torn pair of black lace panties—the other just barely dangling from her foot, garter-less stockings no longer taut at the tops of her thighs, and a little uneven.

Next to her on the bed was a phone and a tube of lubricant.

Between her legs was a dildo larger than anything I had ever seen her use, stretching the swollen outer lips of her hairless cunt into a taut upside-down V, her inflamed clit at the apex.

As she bottomed out with a sob, and began to withdraw this monster cock—the thinner flesh of her inner lips came into view, a deeper red, clinging to the dildo, as if reluctant to let it go—a second, only slightly smaller, shaft emerged from the shiny-slick crease of her ass.

Something else she had never let me do to her, something that, as far as I knew, she had never done to herself in the past either.

She opened her eyes then, saw me in the doorway, gave an animal growl or grunt of anger and surprise that interrupted her litany but blended perfectly with the chaos of her breathing, the rough music of her sounds. Holding my gaze, she continued to withdraw the twin-shafted dildo, making little strangled sounds of what must have been a combination of anguish and pleasure.

When perhaps seven inches had emerged, she paused for just a second or two of quick, shallow panting. She closed her eyes, gave a deep groan, began to thrust back in, her eyes bugging out for a moment, then going heavy-lidded again.

A quick, scratchy, genderless, unintelligible phrase issued from the phone on the bed, and she pulled up as she continued to bear down, briefly changing the angle, mashing the top side of the dildo into her clit which made her cry out.

When she started to speak again she was quieter, not quite whispering, sounded like she was in a trance.

"Mommy's boyfriend," she murmured—in fear, in reverence, in joy?—"*owns* her."

I couldn't tell whether she was in ecstasy or despair; her voice was colored with both awe and resignation.

"Mommy's pussy and Mommy's ass," she moaned, "they *belong* to her boyfriend. Mommy's pussy is *only* for her boyfriend."

There was another sound from the phone.

"Mommy can't even touch *herself* without permission," she said hoarsely, eyes open now and glassy, focused on the ceiling.

There was a third sound, and her hips shuddered, her legs opening wider for the twin prongs that she was pressing relentlessly into herself. Her mouth gaped then closed like a fish out of water, a trickle of saliva at each corner; a red flush bloomed at her cleavage, rising quickly to engulf her face; sweat broke out on her forehead; tears streamed down her cheeks.

"Mommy's boyfriend—" she gulped and sobbed as two or three, flash-fast orgasms shot through her— "he can *give*— Mommy's pussy away— he can *sell* Mommy's ass— he can, he can, he *can. . .*"

I don't know why I quietly closed the door then, stood there in the hallway listening silently, as daylight faded, as the stain of pre-cum on the front of my slacks expanded steadily—from the size of a quarter to the size of a teacup saucer—as my wife, never calling herself anything other than "Mommy," abjectly and completely gave herself over to the pleasure and the pain of the scratchy dictates which continued to issue from her phone.

It seemed the polite thing to do.

81

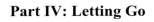

**Part IV: Letting Go**

## Chapter Eleven: Letting Go

I'd gotten home first and I was making dinner—I would have done that whenever I got home; it was both one of my official chores and also something that I enjoyed doing—chopping onions, my eyes a little primed, looking out the window, across our small backyard, light fading, music piped from the living room into the speakers in the kitchen, shuffling through a not-entirely-random mix.

Song from The Band came on: "Twilight," that weird amalgam of Southern blues, reggae, those gorgeous harmonies.

I kept moving through what I had to do, utensils and food, scraps and plates, combining and sorting, chopping and grating, dinner coming together like a puzzle.

The lyrics were snowflakes—or maybe hail—around me, always not quite making sense, always making eerily *perfect* sense. You're insensitive if you don't understand what they mean; you're crazy if you think they're referring directly to you.

I was making chili, so the peppers, the onion, the garlic—I add in shallots, as well; honey sometimes, too—they were all working on my nose, my sinuses, my eyes.

*The lyrics were about light and loneliness.*

Of course my eyes were tearing; that was just chemistry.

Of course that made my nose run; that was just anatomy.

*Light and loneliness.*

And then, for some reason, I wasn't chopping anything anymore.

And I couldn't see properly, the backyard haloed, refracted, and obscured through the sheet of tears streaming down my face.

And it wasn't the onion, the garlic, the chilies, or the shallots.

I was just sobbing and I didn't know why.

The waning of the light?

The fear—the inevitability—of being alone?

The harmonies, the rhythm, some shard of memory or longing or lost hope or promise?

The pain of aging—or of simply *continuing*—the dark, threatening shadow of age and decline?

*I hate crying.*

We're not supposed to do it, men.

Maybe if you're a soldier or a cop, maybe if you're a firefighter, maybe if you've really *earned* it.

But most of us—day-to-day?—we're not supposed to do it.

I don't *believe* that; but it's in my bones.

I heard, but didn't quite register the click of her heels on the kitchen floor, so I didn't jump when she touched me, chin on my shoulder from behind, hand on the small of my back.

If the fact that she'd found me in the kitchen crying was a surprise—or a disappointment—she gave no sign.

"Oh!" she said, in a sympathetic tone that seemed entirely genuine, "my poor little boy!" her fingers lightly tracing the tears that were running down my cheeks.

"Come," she said, taking my hand.

I hesitated, in confusion; I had dinner to finish.

"No," she said, shaking her head. "*That's* not important. You just come with me."

Before sitting on the couch, she took off the high heels she had worn to work, undid the top button or two on her blouse, and in one of those odd, fast, magical, gymnastic maneuvers that women do, twisting this and unclipping that, pulled her bra out of her sleeve to drop unceremoniously on the floor.

She patted the space next to herself when she sat down and I complied.

She pulled my head gently down to her chest, and I had a momentary panic that she wanted to nurse and completely infantilize me.

I may have made inarticulate sounds of concern and resistance, but she just softly *shushed* me, landed my ear on the pillow of her breasts, my nose somewhere between her cleavage and the hollow of her throat.

Her scent was *end-of-the-day*: faded cleansers and perfumes and deodorants; perspiration and frustration and relief; some hint of lunch and co-workers and someone else's cigarette.

I couldn't stop crying.

I couldn't explain.

*The lyrics were about light and loneliness.*

But she didn't ask what was wrong.

*Was I hurt or scared or tired?*

*Had something happened?*

And she didn't say it was going to be okay.

*That horrible, empty platitude—why should* anything *be okay?*

*Why would lying about it be comforting?*

*Why do we* do *that to children—and to each other?*

She just stroked my hair and the back of my neck, leaning down occasionally to bestow a soft kiss on my forehead or my cheek.

"*I know,*" was all she said, over and over, as she cradled me, as I continued to cry, and she said it with a depth and a sincerity and a level of flat conviction that I found *utterly* believable, an oddly soothing balm.

When I couldn't cry anymore, something in me emptied or dry—or *satisfied?*—she cradled me still, stroking and murmuring and kissing and gently rocking.

When I finally tried to sit up, she let me get part way there, but continued to hold me.

Like emerging from sleep, a little disoriented and confused, I struggled for a moment to slip back into waking reality, clearing my throat, rubbing my face.

"I should. . ." I gestured vaguely toward the kitchen.

*"No,"* she said, shaking her head and pursing her lips just a little, as if for show. "My little boy has had a difficult day. We'll just order out for pizza."

I didn't have the strength, or the words, to thank her.

Clearly, I didn't have to; she already knew.

### Chapter Twelve: Apologizing to Mrs. Garber

I had always found my wife's friend Deanna a little disconcerting, though I could never quite put my finger on why.

She was ten years or so older than us: dark hair and eyes, a somewhat intense gaze; she had two kids, ten and twelve; her body showed this, a somewhat bigger woman anyway, a little softer around the edges, ample breasts.

When she followed my wife into our kitchen late one Friday afternoon, I was a little surprised to see her.

"Look who I bumped into at the library!" my wife said brightly.

I nodded in greeting.

Deanna said my name in response. My full name—as she always did, never my nickname.

"Offer me a glass of wine," Deanna said, "I'm never going to turn *that* down."

She was a little dressed up for a weekday afternoon: dark skirt to her knees over stockings and flats; a dark blue blouse, cleavage and the lacy edges of an industrial-strength black bra visible; a single strand of pearls.

"PTA meeting," she said, noticing me noticing.

"Why don't you get us a couple of glasses and open a bottle of Cabernet?" my wife said.

I nodded hurriedly.

When she asked me to do anything, it always slightly flustered me.

It was harder and harder to keep a clear separation between the day-to-day and who and what we were privately—and now she was adopting a tone, in the house, but in front of someone else, that sparked a little shimmer of fear in me.

I uncorked a bottle, brought it to the table with three wine glasses.

"Oh no!" my wife laughed, as though I had done something silly. "I don't think *you* should be drinking," she said. "Well," she seemed to reconsider, "I guess we can put grape juice in your glass—if you want to join us?"

"Okay . . . ?" I said, uncertainly, turning toward the refrigerator to get the juice.

If Deanna thought anything strange about this, she gave no sign.

I filled their glasses with wine, mine with juice; Deanna and I sat.

"You know," my wife said, getting up, "I'm just going to dash upstairs, take off these shoes. My feet have been *killing* me today!"

She left the room.

Deanna raised her glass, and I reflexively followed suit.

"*Cin Cin!*" she said.

Clinking glasses, we both took a sip.

"Does it chafe?" Deanna asked evenly.

"I'm sorry does *what*. . ?"

I started to take a second sip of juice.

"That little cock constrictor she has you in," Deanna said, her tone perfectly neutral and conversational, "does it chafe?" I almost choked on my juice. "Because that *can* be a problem."

I coughed, trying to get my breath back.

She *knew*?

"Of *course* I know," Deanna said, answering the unspoken question. "I'm the one who trained *her* to train *you*."

I was dizzy again, off balance.

"Well we should check," Deanna said firmly. "Be a *good* boy and stand up."

I obeyed without thinking, blood roaring in my ears; she knew the right words.

"Pants and shorts down to your knees," she said.

"I can't. . ."

"You *are* going to be a *good* boy for me, aren't you?"

Fumbling with my belt, I did it quickly—it wasn't happening; it wasn't real—shoving pants and shorts down as one, exposing my shaved crotch, my imprisoned cock, trying not to let my hands shake.

Making a sound of approval, she reached out, cupping and squeezing my balls, first gently, then more firmly; eliciting a tremulous whine from my throat, she let go.

"*What do you think you're doing!*" my wife shouted from the kitchen doorway, making me jump. "You are a *very* bad boy! How *dare* you expose yourself to Mrs. Garber like that!"

Deanna shook her head, as if in disappointment.

"He said he had something he wanted to show me, then he just stood up and pulled down his pants. I've never—" she paused and seemed to think, "well *almost never* seen anything like this."

"I am *terribly* sorry," my wife said. "I can assure you he *will* be punished."

Walking fully into the room, she picked up her wine glass from the table, drained almost half of it in a single gulp, as if fortifying herself.

Deanna picked up her glass and sipped from it pensively.

I stood frozen to the spot.

"No—" I floundered. "I *wasn't*— She *made* me—"

"*What?* Are you calling Mrs. Garber a liar?"

"Well," Deanna said, reaching for the wine bottle and re-filling both of their glasses, "this is just insult-to-injury. I don't know *how* we make *this* right."

"He will apologize, I assure you. He will be punished, and he will apologize," my wife said with crisp certainty.

Deanna shrugged dismissively.

"I'll believe it when I *see* it," she said, her voice lower now, more forceful.

They stood silently for a few moments, sipping, as if in thought.

My heart hammered in my chest as they finished their second glasses of wine.

"Alright," my wife said to me firmly, "you march right into the living room and kneel with your head on the couch and your bottom in the air, and you wait for us."

I started simultaneously walking and pulling my pants back up.

Deanna looked away and murmured something I couldn't hear.

"*Stop!*" my wife said. "You put your pants back down around your knees, where they were, and march into the living room that way. I did *not* give you permission to pull them up."

I complied, feeling hobbled and juvenile, knees creaking, as I knelt in front of the couch, cheeks burning, as I leaned forward and lay my face on the cushion.

From the kitchen, I heard the sound of chairs scraping against the floor, the bottle, the glasses, muted conversation punctuated by the occasional soft laugh.

It must have been at least another twenty minutes before they followed me into the living room, the punishment hairbrush visible in my wife's hand.

"Mrs. Garber has generously agreed to forgive you," she said. "And you are *very* lucky. This could have gotten you into *really big trouble!* Serious things happen to *bad* little boys who go around showing people their wee-wees. Are *you* a bad little boy?"

I struggled to find the right answer, my head spinning, the question suddenly serious to me.

*I am bad,* I thought.

*I want to touch girls, I want to steal things, I want to hurt people, even kill them; I'm not just bad, really, I'm evil, dangerous, fraudulent, untrustworthy, simply unworthy.*

That was the deep truth, wasn't it?

Outside the living room.

Outside any game or role playing.

The horrifying reality.

"I'm— I was— I don't . . . *know,*"

"You don't *know?*" she said, as if in disbelief. "Mommy is very, *very* disappointed to hear that. I thought I was teaching you better than that." She folded her arms across her breasts, huffed. "You are going to have to apologize *very* personally."

Deanna stepped over me to sit down on the couch, one of her legs on either side of me, lifted the hem of her skirt into her lap. She wore no panties, had a thicket of dark, coarse pubic hair.

Looking down at me, she patted the hair, spoke in that familiar tone you would use to address a child.

"It *is* a furry kitty, isn't it?" she said, smiling. "Mama doesn't trim the shrubbery. *Her* little boy just has to work his way through. But he gets *lots and lots* of practice. Just like I bet your Mommy makes sure that *you* get lots of practice, doesn't she?"

93

My throat was too dry for me to answer . . . *Oh but Mistress Mommy's beautiful, fragrant, smoothly shaven, cunny, that was so, so different from—*

"Mrs. Garber asked you a question!"

"Yes . . . Yes, Mrs. Garber, Mistress Mommy makes sure I get lots of practice."

*"That's good!"* she cried enthusiastically. "Because, while your Mommy gives you a good . . . long . . . *hard* spanking, you are going to apologize directly to my kitty. Do you understand me young man?"

"Yes, Mrs. Garber," I whispered.

"That'll be more discreet, anyway," she said to me, as if in confidence. "It will help muffle your crying!"

At that, she swiftly and tightly knotted the fingers of her right hand in my hair, jerked me forward, slamming my face into her densely tangled bush, just as I felt Mistress Mommy steady herself—the cool, light touch of her splayed fingers on the small of my back—and then that first tremendous blow of the brush on my bottom.

I screamed, but the sound was indeed muffled, just like the strangled cries for help that we can't quite get out in nightmares. With Mrs. Garber's large soft thighs clamped tightly against my ears, I sounded far away even from myself.

I *felt,* as much as heard, her grunt, the power of the blow transmitted through me, turned into vibration.

My pain: Mistress Mommy's pleasure.

Mrs. Garber opened her thighs for a moment, raised my head.

"Oh look! He's crying already! Why don't we try practicing your apology?"

"I— what? I'm . . . Mrs. Garber, I'm sorry that I showed you my wee-wee?"

"He doesn't really seem *sure,*" she sighed in resignation.

94

To me, she whispered, as if we were co-conspirators, "use your *nose* first—to poke through—*then* your tongue. And make sure to pay a lot of attention to the little red button."

She winked at me.

I started to nod, but that motion was lost in the downward thrust as she pushed my face back into her hairy lap; Mistress Mommy swatted me again; Mrs. Garber grunted in pleasure.

This went on for at least half an hour: one, two, or three swats in succession, as I desperately struggled to reach—to *find*—her clit; pulled up to apologize with greater and greater precision and detail; pushed back down to start again.

Until finally—my crying constant, my face scratched from her wiry hair; Mrs. Garber's grunting becoming a faster, deeper, steady rhythm, accompanied by a more and more powerful squeezing of my head between her thighs; Mistress Mommy beginning to sound like a winded tennis player, giving a little cry of effort with each stroke—there came the relief of that final seizure, Deanna knotting both hands in my hair, pounding my face down, thrusting her groin up, giving that throaty growl I *desperately* needed to hear (would this—it *had* to!—*finally* end?) as she came.

As if she were surprised—grudgingly admitting something to Mistress Mommy, as if she were acknowledging that I had passed some trial, or that she had lost a bet—she managed just a few distinct words.

"Uhhhhh, *he is!* uhhhh a . . . *Goooood* Boooy!"

## Chapter Thirteen: Mommy Makes a Popsicle

So she *had* been trained.

And trained by *Deanna!*

I struggled in the days that followed—in the *daze* that followed!—to understand what this meant, my first reaction being that this was *not* private.

Hadn't *that* been one of the fundamental things to which Mistress Mommy had agreed at the outset?

But that idea quickly fell down in at least two ways.

First, she had said—I'd heard her say; I'd tacitly accepted—"at least for now."

She'd said it more softly, a quiet pigtail to her telling me that "of course!" we would keep things private. But there had been no deviousness or concealment. She was not being dishonest; she was acting within the letter of what we had agreed together.

Second, it was now clear that this had *never* been completely private. Deanna, of course, had known even before *I* knew, even before we *started.*

Finally, there was just no arguing—what would the point have been, anyway?

It was done, an accomplished fact that nothing could ever erase.

One of Mistress Mommy's mantras, had become, "Mommies can explain *if they want to*, but they *never*," she would frown—as if the very idea she was about to broach was so incomprehensible as to be a little annoying, an irresponsible waste of Mommy's time to even *consider* a response—purse her lips, furrow her eyebrows, shake her head gravely back and forth, "they *never* have to justify themselves."

Mommy didn't *do* justification.

And, on the rare occasion that she explained something, it was usually after the fact, and often an explanation she made *me* give, having set up and run me through some important "lesson," to which she would—once in a while—refer back.

Experience, de-briefing, lesson, quiz, reinforcement.

Was *that* part of her training?

Her training in how to train *me*?

After a few days, I would come to take some solace in the fact that the arrangement of *Deanna's* household had been invisible to me—for years, it seemed likely—her husband just an average Joe.

They had children.

And it was clear in retrospect that the kids knew nothing of any odd goings on in their parents' marriage; they were certainly old enough by then to have some awareness of difference or deviance.

Whatever else Deanna was, she was obviously extraordinarily adept at being discreet.

To outward appearances, anyway.

Within the confines of the *Mommy World*—where she was *what exactly?* certainly a highly skilled *Program Trainer*—she was clearly capable of *throwing the switch,* unleashing herself in the same ways that I had been watching my wife change, fluid, powerful, unselfconscious, regularly limning and toying with the edge of savagery.

When Deanna had finally cum to her satisfaction, I was perfunctorily praised and dismissed to the bathroom.

My face was already red from the repeated scratching against her profuse, wild, and coarse pubic hair; it could get no redder as I scrubbed, repeatedly and furiously, to try to remove her scent.

*It wasn't fair!*

The phrase was unsuppressible.

It tore through my mind in an endlessly repeating stream, over and over and over again, louder and louder and louder, until I realized I was shouting it, in full tantrum.

Having made no decision to cause a confrontation, I was almost surprised to see my hand reach out for the bathroom doorknob, felt the giddy, frightened anticipation of striding down the hallway and back into the living room.

The door had been locked from the outside.

A latch had been installed?

*When?*

How had I not *noticed* this?

I was struck silent in astonishment, but the phrase welled up in me again, unstoppable, and, as I wailed it, I windmilled my arms, pounding futilely on the door.

I have no idea how long that went on.

I must have fallen asleep on the bathroom floor, starting awake to Mistress Mommy's soft fingers on my still-red face.

Through the window, I could see that it was dark outside.

She was squatting in the doorway, in her fluffy white bathrobe, her big white panties visible underneath, with the characteristic wet spot of arousal.

I looked briefly up at her and could see *both* of her nipples, fully erect, her breasts hanging so beautifully over me, her robe only loosely tied.

"No peeking at Mommy," she cautioned softly, only the slightest edge of warning in her voice. "Let's not be mad at each other anymore, okay?"

I wouldn't answer her.

She continued to stroke my face, silently, for several long minutes, making no move to close her robe. Squatting as she was, so close, the scent of her cunt was strong.

Finally, she leaned over further and kissed me, grazing, as she almost never did anymore, my lips before landing tenderly on my hot cheek.

"Mrs. Garber marked you with her scent, didn't she?" she said almost inaudibly.

In sympathy?

With a tinge of territorial resentment?

"I don't feel well," I muttered, sullenly.

She sighed.

"Alright then," she said, standing, gathering her robe more tightly. "Go to your room, get undressed, and we'll get you ready for bed."

I obeyed, taking my clothes off, throwing them on the floor, getting into bed and curling up in fetal position under just a sheet.

I might have just started to drowse off when she came in and turned on the light, stood in the middle of the room surveying, magazines by the side of the bed, clothes on the floor.

"You know you're supposed to either put away your clothes or put them in the hamper," she said, in her disappointed voice.

"I don't *feel* well," I said plaintively.

"Be *very* careful not to yell at Mommy," she said evenly. "You know that's rude."

"I'm . . . I'm sorry Mistress Mommy. I don't feel well," I said, this time more meekly.

"Alright," she said, her tone resigned but with a slight tremor to it that I couldn't quite read.

She briskly picked up all the clothing on the floor and stuffed it into the hamper, left the room, the light still on.

She was back very quickly, a pair of medical exam gloves in one hand, a little transparent plastic pouch in the other, inside of which I could see multiple tubes of ointment, a prominent jar of Vaseline, several thermometers.

"On your tummy," she said crisply. "Mommy will take care of you."

"Wait, *no*— I don't—"

"We *have* to find out if you're really sick," she said, raising her eyebrows and her tone, as if in surprise that I might object. "Mommies can get in *very* big trouble if they don't take proper care of their little boys," she said. "And I don't think you want to be naughty again today after the spanking Mrs. Garber and I had to give you this afternoon, do you? Your bottom must really hurt already. Come on, be Mommy's good boy and lie on your belly."

I did as she told me.

"Now reach back and hold your bottom open for Mommy."

She left me like that for a few moments.

I turned my face to the wall, heard the pouch being unzipped—the sharp sound of a jar, the light tinkle of glass as she put the Vaseline and the thermometer on my night table. I heard the sounds of her putting on the gloves, pulling at them, snapping them—the sound of the jar being popped open and then the greasy petroleum jelly aroma hit me.

She knelt by the side of the bed and I felt a dollop of the lubricant land right on my anus.

At first she was very delicate, barely the tip of one finger making small, light, lazy, slow circles; once in a while she exerted just the slightest pressure, dead center, with hardly any penetration at all.

She nuzzled the back of my neck and I shivered.

"Mommy has to make sure that you're *nice* and greasy," she said breathily, "so nothing hurts her good little boy."

I gave a whimper, whether in resistance or gratitude, I couldn't say.

Her other gloved hand gently roamed my red and sore buttocks, exploring.

"That was a *very* hard spanking Mommy and Mrs. Garber had to give you," she said, in a slightly childish voice. Then, "*here* we go," and her finger was in up to the first knuckle.

She pulsed it slowly—which I hated, which I loved.

Then to the second knuckle, then all the way, pulling it almost all the way out, sliding it fully back in.

"It feels like you have a very swollen . . . *walnut* in your bottom," she said thoughtfully.

There was no way for me to answer.

She added a second finger, stretching me, but not quite to the point of discomfort; I could feel pre-cum steadily dripping onto the sheet beneath me.

When she penetrated me with the third finger, it hurt. "Mommy—*Ouch!*"

"*Shush, shush, shush,*" she said hurriedly, her other hand pressing down on the small of my back, restricting my movement, pushing the chastity cage harder against the mattress, and against my frustrated, imprisoned cock. "It's okay, it's *okay*," she said. "Mommy's *almost* done— and . . . *there,*" she withdrew all of her fingers and turned again to the night table.

The glass thermometer was cold against the swollen walnut of my prostate.

"Mommy will be right back," she murmured, turning off the light as she left the room.

I heard the scrape of the night table drawer in what had become her room, then the faint buzz of one of her smaller vibrators, almost immediately followed by three quick grunts—*unnh! unnh!! unnnh!!!*—of the sort you might make hammering a difficult nail.

They didn't sound like noises of satisfaction; the vibrator clicked off; the drawer scraped again.

She came back down the hall, turned on the light, plucked out the thermometer, wiped it off with a tissue and held it up to read it.

"It's . . . ninety-eight point . . . seven," she said. "Well. That's *good!* You're not sick."

I made an inarticulate grumpy sound and she tousled my hair.

"Bedtime then! Let's shave your wee-wee to get you ready. Go to the bathroom; Mommy will be there in a minute."

I hesitated.

This was wrong.

She had shaved me just the day before.

"*Scoot!*" she said. "Listen to Mommy."

With an uncharacteristic reluctance, I did.

As she shaved me, she talked to me slowly, in the kind of slightly distant, slightly disjointed way one does when the conversation is punctuating some activity which takes thought or concentration.

"Do you *remember*," she said, slowly, as she wiped away the remnants of the shaving cream, "when you wanted to be," she paused, finding a little jot she had missed on my thigh, "Mommy's *dildie?*"

My heart lurched.

"Yes, Mistress Mommy," I said hoarsely.

She was oiling my cock as though in preparation for locking it back up again as usual, concentrating intently on that task.

"Well," she said, massaging my aching balls, "Mommy was *thinking,*" dabbing at the underside of the head of my cock, "*maybe,*" now greasing the whole shaft with a little more force than usual, "we just might," she looked up at my face, "*try* that *again.*"

She hadn't used the baby oil she always used to grease me.

What she had used smelled different and a little funny.

The idea of fucking her—how long had it been?—was overwhelmingly exciting.

But I was conflicted.

Locked up, teased, denied a full, satisfying orgasm for *such* a long time, I didn't *think*, I *knew*, there was no way that I was going to be able to last more than a couple of strokes.

It wouldn't be satisfying for her; it would be humiliating for me.

For the second time that day, her robe was loose, as she sat on the edge of the tub, working on me. Looking down to meet her gaze, I again saw *both* of her nipples.

I thought I felt my cock throb in response, it was still rock hard and pointing skyward.

But then I realized: *I couldn't actually feel my cock at all!*

Looking down, I could *see* that she had four fingers on the top of the shaft, her thumb just under the head, and that she was, very delicately, stroking and squeezing me.

*I couldn't feel that.*

She rinsed off the facecloth again, fully swabbed my cock twice.

"Mrs. Garber," she said, again concentrating on her task, "felt just a *little* guilty about how much her big hairy cunny scratched up your face this afternoon, which," she concentrated her attention just below the head again, as if she had seen a spot of dust, "is *very* unusual. *Guilt* is not something that tends to . . . *trouble* her."

She paused, as if to inspect her work.

"She gave Mommy a present," she continued brightly. "A tube of this *magical* ointment," she grinned, wolfishly.

"And *that's* why you can't feel your wee-wee! And *that's* why," she said lowering her tone, "you are going to be a simply *wonderful dildie* for Mommy tonight. Aren't you happy she gave us this treat?"

I could only nod slowly.

She led me back to what had once been our room, had me lie on my back in what had once been our bed, and rode me like I was a bronco, though she did most of the bucking.

For almost an hour, she sat astride me with her bathrobe fully open but still on; when she lay down on my chest—the achingly exciting feeling of her breasts pressed full up against me—the robe covered both of us like a blanket. At one point, she pulled it fully over our heads, riding and grinding on me in darkness—was she imagining that I was someone else?

It got so hot under there, so sweaty, that, at one point, she muttered, "You're giving *Mommy* a fever— such a— *unhhh!*— such a— *good*— boy. *Such a good* dildie *for Mommy!*"

I could feel her body, smell her, taste her, thrill to the sounds she made; my cock remained steel-hard—and dead numb.

When she was done, she climbed off me and rested, lay my head on her shoulder, her arms up, bracketing her pillow as if in surrender.

"You were very, *very* good, helping Mommy with her needs like that," she said, almost shyly. "Would you like this to be your special treat now and then? Mommy does like a warm and . . . *fleshy dildie* sometimes, instead of that big, old," a quick tremor went through her, "*bumpy* one."

"My wee-wee hurts really bad," I whispered.

Not the answer I wanted to give; I didn't really know what answer she wanted to hear.

Her voice took on a note of clinical concern.

"Is it your wee-wee that hurts," she asked slowly, "or is it," her *childish-sexy* vocabulary had some gaps in it, "is it your little . . . marbles?"

"It's— I *think* it's my . . . *marbles,* but there's something else, like it hurts in my bottom."

"Did Mommy hurt your bottom with her fingernails?" she asked, her voice conveying sincere concern. "Or did Mommy stretch your bottom a little too much?"

"No— It's— I *think* it's that 'swollen walnut' Mommy said she felt."

Would she put all of those things together?

Maybe allow this *once-in-a-while-treat* to be dispensed with me experiencing full sensation?

Would she give me a kind of *medical exemption,* now and then, to reduce the pressure on my prostate?

"Ohhhhh . . ." she said, as if in sudden realization. "Mommy understands. You go back to the bathroom and Mommy will be there in a minute."

I had no idea what she was going to do, but I almost skipped there.

I was standing in the tub, when she came in, but she laughed and said, "No, come here to Mommy."

She doubled up a fluffy bath towel and put it on the floor.

"Put your knees there," she said, "and lay your head on the side of the tub."

"Wait— *What?"*

"Don't *question* Mommy," she said softly. "Be my *good* boy."

"Put your elbows on the edge, too," she said, when I complied, which somehow had the odd effect of making me point my knees inward, opening myself up more.

106

I heard her snap on just one medical exam glove. She slid a little, red, plastic cereal bowl underneath me and unceremoniously plunged a finger into my still-greasy ass, up to the second knuckle in one stroke, almost out again, then fully in, then immediately a second finger. With the two all the way in, she began to draw them back slowly, pressing down firmly.

I jumped when her fingers reached the far edge of that swollen walnut.

"*There* we are," she said, breathily. "We just have to *milk* you a little, that's all," she leaned forward to kiss the small of my back, "*that's* all."

I smelled the baby oil, and she reached underneath me with her ungloved hand, first rolling my balls around in her palm, then making a ring around the bottom of my shaft with thumb and forefinger, pulling up to just under the crown and oscillating there.

At the same time, she continued to massage my prostate.

Sensation was beginning to return; I felt *something,* and was surprised to see, when I looked underneath myself, that I was releasing a steady trickle into the bowl.

When she seemed to sense that I was getting too excited—sometimes I couldn't stop myself from trying to push against her hand, like a dog humping someone's leg—she would stop the massage, her fingers still deep inside me, the thumb of the other hand just under the head of my cock, the index finger above, pincering and holding tight there for a few moments.

Then the motions, above and below, resumed.

It felt like peeing, the gradual relief of emptying my bladder; but it didn't feel like cumming, this slow stream she milked out of me, until it covered the bottom of the little bowl.

"O-kaay . . ." she said, "*almost* done," slowing, then stopping, as the flow dwindled to a few intermittent drops,

107

then withdrawing her fingers from me, letting go of my cock—sensation was coming back fully now and it hurt; she had fucked me raw, though I hadn't been able to feel it—she kissed me again on the small of my back.

"You've been a very *good* boy," she murmured. "Thank you for telling Mommy what you needed. Mommy will be sure to do everything she needs to, to keep her little boy nice and healthy."

She stood, removed the glove, threw it away, washed her hands.

"Now," she said, as if to herself. "What did we do with your towel and your bowl of ice?"

She hadn't told me to get them ahead of time.

"It's okay," she said, brightly, "Mommy will get them."

I didn't plan it; I didn't think about it; I was doing it before I fully processed my own action.

She went down the hall to the kitchen and I began *furiously* jerking off, steadying myself with one hand on the edge of the tub; the other hand must have been a blur on my already raw and abraded cock.

I stayed hard; I felt some pleasure, along with the pain of what I was doing—the pain rising—but I couldn't cum.

"*Ohhhh,*" she said, standing in the doorway watching me, the bowl of ice in one hand, "my towel" in the other, her tone with a slightly sad, *isn't-that-cute* lilt to it.

I stopped, out of breath, gulping and gasping, mortified and frustrated, my cock throbbing, actually bleeding a little bit.

"I— Oh, *God!*— I just need— I just need to— I just *need*—"

She sat down on the toilet seat, put her chin in her hand.

"Mommy is *so* sorry," she said. "You don't really understand do you? Once Mommy has *milked* you? You can't *have* any cummies. You can *try*—Mommy is a little upset that you tried like *that*; it looks like you might have actually hurt your wee-wee; it was a little naughty and nasty of you—but . . . *no*," she shook her head, as if in regret, "there's nothing left to come out, is there?"

"It's okay, it's okay," she added hurriedly. "Mommy's not going to punish you for what you did. *Not this time* . . ."

She sighed.

"You *were* a *very* good *dildie* for Mommy tonight," she said, a little dreamily.

"You were a *very* good boy, the way you helped Mommy with her needs. But I think we can both *see* that when we make your wee-wee into a popsicle like that, it's really not *good* for you, it's really not *healthy. Can't we see that?* Isn't that the *lesson* that we've learned? I know you *love* to help Mommy—and that's, oh it's *adorable!*— but you really look sad and frustrated now. I don't want you to be sad like this. So is the lesson that we won't do any more popsicles?"

My cock was still hard, sensation almost fully back, looking a little like a cat had scratched it up, the stinging almost unbearable; the *pressure* had been relieved, but the fever pitch of my thwarted *desire* had only increased; I had the horrible realization that the numbing of the ice, so she could secure me again, was actually going to be something of a *relief.*

"Yes, Mistress Mommy," I whispered in resignation.

"Good boy! It was nice of Mrs. Garber to give us this treat, though, don't you think? We'll have to have you write her a thank you note."

**Part V:  After**

## Chapter Fourteen: The Nice Man

It had been a year, almost exactly.

I sat on the edge of what used to be my bed, trying not to cry.

I had answered the door naked, except for my chastity device, had haltingly invited the Nice Man in, brought him to the bedroom, all as Mistress Mommy had instructed.

She stood before me in a floor-length, filmy, black négligé—*so* different from the big cotton panties, the chaste nightgowns, the fluffy white bathrobe she wore for me—and gently stroked my hair.

The Nice Man waited in the hall.

"It's upsetting," she said softly, "and scary too, isn't it?" she cooed, just a little tremble in her voice.

"Yes, Mistress Mommy," I whispered.

"But we know," she paused, a finger under my chin, so that I had to raise my face and look at her. "We *know* this is what we have to do, don't we?"

"*Why?*" I managed, my breathing increasingly erratic.

I was trembling and dizzy, not sure what was fear and revulsion, what was passion and excitement.

"We know that you are only allowed to use your wee-wee on special occasions," she said, in her reasonable voice, simply making a logical point.

113

I tried to nod, but her finger kept my head steady.

"And we *know,*" she said, her voice getting huskier as she spoke, "that Mommy has . . . *needs.*"

I didn't try to nod, just blinked in acknowledgement.

"And you are *very* good—such a *good boy*—at licking Mommy's cunny, getting Mommy her vibrator, helping Mommy with her *dildie.*"

Another blink.

"And why does Mommy use her *dildie?*"

I closed my eyes for a moment, then managed to croak, "because it's better than my wee-wee. It's bigger . . . and it always stays hard for Mistress Mommy."

"That's right, *that's* right," she cooed, her hand moving up to tenderly stroke my hair. Then, taking a half-step forward, her hands on my shoulders, she pushed me gently to my knees, then pressed my head to her belly.

"Can you *smell* how excited Mommy is?" she whispered huskily, pressing my head, painfully, a little lower, my forehead to her navel, my nose just above her swollen, shaven cleft, visible through the filmy black fabric.

I nodded my head against her belly and could feel the excited trembling of *her* breathing, the rising thrum of her heartbeat; she swallowed and found a more controlled rhythm, continuing in the same whisper.

"Mommy loves her little boy so much, so *so* much. But sometimes Mommy needs a *man.* And that's what the Nice Man is here for today. That's why Mrs. Garber is letting Mommy *borrow* him. To help Mommy with her . . ." the word caught in her throat, "*needs.*"

I *could* smell her.

The négligé opened just slightly and I could *see* the lips of her cunt redden, pulsing in time to the hammering of her heart, swelling further, beginning to part, as if in hunger and anticipation.

"You need to go out into the hall now, and ask the Nice Man to come in and fuck Mommy," she said. "You *need* to do this," she reiterated, lifting my head from her belly, looking straight into my eyes. "You *need* to be Mommy's *good* little boy. Isn't that right?"

For a year now, she had been calling me that, saying it after I came in her hand, after I licked her palm and fingers carefully and thoroughly clean, after every orgasm I gave her.

It still terrified, mortified, and disgusted me.

I felt ashamed and frightened and lost.

But I also felt protected and found and . . . *loved.*

*Even now?*

Somehow—kneeling, looking furtively at the body she both denied and allowed me, a kind of rationing, really; my knees barely grazing her feet, always hyper-aware of any time I touched any part of her; lost in the tangle of her scents: her perfume, the soapy smell of her skin, the increasingly strong aroma of her arousal—I *did* feel loved.

She had been giving me pleasure in the—utterly bizarre series of—ways that I wanted, or, as she had said, *needed.*

Shouldn't she be given the same gift?

If she had a need—if she had a *hunger*—that I couldn't fully sate, why wouldn't I do everything I could (was there *anything* I wouldn't do?) to help satisfy that need for her?

There was still that single button that I could push.

Perhaps insanely, I believed that, if I said "stop," she would stop.

But what would that mean?

What would happen *then?*

How would we unwind the past year and where would we end up?

And what did I *want* things to be like, *really?*

115

It had occurred to me, perhaps a month earlier, that while what we were doing was a particularly intense and deep form of age play, in a lot of ways, I was like a Victorian wife: as long as I was obedient in certain large but clearly defined spheres, I was safe and loved and protected.

That my spouse had a variety of needs which I had neither the capacity nor even perhaps the desire to fully satisfy logically meant that some outside help or activity was reasonable and appropriate.

In fact *that* was *fair*.

"I'll go get the Nice Man," I managed.

"Such a *good* boy," she murmured.

My legs were a little unsteady as I walked the necessary few feet, my constricted cock pulsing against the confines of the chastity device in frustrated desire.

Opening the door, I stepped just barely into the hallway, where he was leaning against the wall, looking at his shoes.

"Please come in," I said.

Mistress Mommy stood near the head of the bed, her négligé open nearly an inch now, from neckline to floor.

"Bobby!" she said brightly, "thank you so much for doing this," as if she were addressing the lawn boy—which in some ways she was.

"Why don't you get undressed so we can get started?"

He did so quickly, his cock a long, thick, bobbing pointer to his flat belly.

*"Lit-tle bo-oy . . . ?"* Mistress Mommy crooned, sing-song. "Come kneel in front of Mommy, again."

I tried to completely shut off thought.

*Just obey.*

She opened the négligé fully, gracing me with an unobstructed view of her soft, slightly rounded, belly, smooth, muscled thighs, her breasts swaying above me, *areolae* crinkled, dark, and tight, nipples erect; the petals

116

of that flower that led to her powerful core parted even further now, at the top, where her red and engorged clit pulsed; she was *visibly* wet, her inner thighs sheened, as if with baby oil, a drop like a tear slowly tracing a path that I desperately longed to follow with my tongue.

"Be a *good* boy and ask the Nice Man to fuck Mommy, and Mommy will let you lick her cunny to get her ready."

"Please fuck my Mommy," I said, softly and quickly, not looking up, expecting her to correct me, make me look up, have me say it differently.

But instead she twined the fingers of both of her hands—painfully—in my hair, bringing my face down into that gorgeous, swollen, fragrant, wetness.

"*Such* a good boy," she growled, the muscles of her thighs twitching as she sought to remain standing.

I was hopelessly and ecstatically lost.

*She was the universe.*

*Nothing else existed.*

"Wait!" she said sharply, after what felt like only a moment, pulling back from me just slightly.

I gently laved the outer folds, the crease of her inner thigh.

"*Don't.* Make. Mommy. Cum," she managed, with difficulty, through gritted teeth, then, as if with some regret, gently pushing my head away, just an inch or so.

She gave a shuddering sigh as she gathered herself, softly stroking my now-wet cheeks.

"You are *such* a good boy," she said quietly, "so *generous*, so thoughtful, so *sensitive*," that beautiful note of deep and genuine gratitude thrilling me.

"Now my good little boy has to go stand in the corner, while the Nice Man takes care of Mommy's needs. *No peeking!* And, if you *stay* good, we can cuddle later."

I went to the corner.

I heard the faint squeak of springs as she got onto the bed.

"You're up, Bobby!" she said, attempting that same bright *praising-the-child* tone, but failing, her voice as quivery as her thighs had been.

The mattress squeaked for a second time.

And louder.

## Chapter Fifteen: After

I don't know how many times she came.

I don't know how long I stood there, my nose not quite in the corner, overpowered by the scent on my face, in a kind of trance, my body numb and distant, aware that my feet hurt, that my neck was getting stiff, that my cock was dripping pre-cum, the sounds of sex loud, vivid, and intense—but somehow not quite real.

She was *utterly* unrestrained.

Nothing too filthy for her to say—nothing too cliché.

The *yes's;* the *no's. Oh, please! Oh, thank you!*

I was terrified at first that the neighbors would hear her screaming, although it wouldn't take long to understand that what they were hearing was passion and not violence.

*What would they think?*

*And was Bobby's car in our driveway?*

Then I was thunderstruck by the realization that she didn't *care* what they thought.

Maybe she even *wanted* them to know, a kind of outing of herself and—by extension—of me.

*But what could I do?*
Which is when the second wave hit me:
*I couldn't.*
*Do.*
*Anything.*
So . . .
*I wasn't. Responsible.*

That rush of relief—and passion and pleasure and gratitude—weakened my knees for a moment and I reached out to the wall to steady myself.

That was the point—*wasn't it?*

That was the starting point, really, what she had said to me on that first strange night when she woke me up— in such a bizarre multiplicity of ways?

That was the molten *core* of what we were doing.

I *hadn't* hit the stop button; I had chosen to accept the primacy of her pleasure.

She could do *anything she wanted to do*: she was the adult.

Adults don't accept the judgment of children; they don't have to accept the judgment of other adults.

They simply live their lives, making decisions, indulging passions, however they see fit.

*No asking.*

*No explaining.*

*No justifying.*

And the life of a child—in a strict but loving household—at my imagined "age," just on the cusp of adolescence, was simple: I didn't have anything to worry about except pleasing Mistress Mommy.

Sometimes that meant eating something disgusting because that was what Mommy wanted, those vile things adults like: the slime of eggplant; nausea-inducing peas; Brussels sprouts that caused actual gagging; the horrific insanity of raw fish (But Mommy, it's *raw! You said* we're *never* supposed to eat things like that raw!).

120

As long as I did that?

Everything was alright.

And when I *didn't* please Mistress Mommy?

Well . . . there was punishment—which clearly filled some need for me as well.

When we had *played?*

She'd rarely been deeply into it.

Whatever we did?

Wasn't her script.

More than that?

It *was* a script.

What we had been doing for the past year didn't feel that way, *at all*; it was different. There was a framework and there were roles, but she was genuinely deciding: what we would do, how we would do it.

And I was accepting this.

We'd both gone deeper and deeper into a weird kind of freedom.

She didn't *care* what *anyone* thought anymore; that was the ultimate freedom.

And the untethering of her desires from any kind of restraint was both gorgeous and horrific, the terrible beauty of watching a lioness stalk, bring down, and joyously dismember an antelope on the savannah.

But—*most* of the time—I wasn't the antelope; I was an awed cub.

I was just a little boy; I had no real guilt or obligation or responsibility—for her actions or for my own; nothing could really be my fault; you can't blame children for being children.

What do we say after all?

*Come on, leave him alone. He's just a kid.*

The last time she came, before thanking Bobby and softly dismissing him—I heard his grunt in response, efficient sounds of him dressing, the bedroom door, quick footfalls down the stairs, the slam of the front door, his car starting (he *had* been in the driveway!) and the fading engine sound as he drove away—it sounded almost like she was crying.

I could tell—I could *hear*—that he had been fucking her from behind, had pushed her flat onto her belly, was slamming into her powerfully and fast, the bed wheezing rhythmically, his thighs slapping her ass, her breathing like sobbing hiccups, as he drove the air from her body, time and time again.

She came with a long, loud, high, keening sound, like a howl of pain that fell to a grunting, ragged shuddering for breath, lying there as he dressed and left, still not able to properly get her air, little moans and sighs and grunts trickling out of her in a stream that took a while to slow.

I was shaking.

When she spoke, her voice was thick, as if she had been sleeping, as if words were an effort, her throat unaccustomed to communication.

"You can turn around now little boy."

She was splayed across the bed on her belly, arms out, hands slightly over her head, hair a tousled mess, her body sheened with sweat, festooned with red and pink marks, scratches, welts, a general blush across her ass.

"Does Mommy look like the Nice Man did a good job taking care of her needs?" she managed thickly.

"Yes, Mistress Mommy," I whispered.

"Yes, he did," she muttered. "Come here, be my *good* boy and cuddle with Mommy."

I walked gingerly to the bed and lay down next to her, facing the edge. She flopped her near arm around my body, found and tweaked one of my nipples, as if seeking a reference point to orient herself, then brought her hand down and closed it around the chastity device.

"Turn toward me, little boy," she murmured, and I did. "I bet your wee-wee *really* hurts in there, doesn't it? Standing there for all that time. Listening to all those

122

funny noises that Mommy and the Nice Man were making."

I nodded against her shoulder.

She let go, took my hand, guided it down, below her belly.

"*Very* gently," she whispered, "the Nice Man really *pounded* Mommy's cunny."

A mixture of her wetness and his cum oozed from her swollen lips.

"Mommy needs her *good* boy," she said softly, gathering the effort to make her voice more authoritative again, "to make her cunny all clean again, before she goes to sleep. Lick it *very* gently, but very thoroughly."

"Mistress Mommy . . ?"

I didn't want to do it; I couldn't say no to her.

"You always eat *your* cummies, don't you?" she said using her reasonable voice.

I nodded against her, a tendril of her sweaty hair across my cheek.

"Well, it doesn't matter whether the cummies are from you or from the Nice Man. Cummies always have to be cleaned up."

Frozen, I felt those little creaks inside; I was about to give in.

I hadn't hit the stop button.

On some level I had known exactly what that would mean.

"And then tomorrow," she said, knowing this would put me over the edge, "we can take out your wee-wee," her voice got slower and softer and more childlike, "we can make sure it's *nice* and *clean*—we'll wash it *extra* well, won't we?—and then you can have *your* cummies. Deal?"

She almost never made it even *sound* like she might be giving a negotiable instruction.

She was offering me the option to say, "no," but not say, "stop."

Was that a *get-out-of-jail-free* card?

Or a *choose-to-remain-submissive* trap?

She was giving me, as well, the—*pleasurable?* in some way, clearly—humiliation of saying, of *having to* say, "yes," which I knew was what would please her, what she wanted to hear.

Even as I softly said, "yes, Mistress Mommy," I could feel her moving my head gently down her body, my torso and limbs following, baggage that had no weight at all.

It didn't feel like I was doing it.

It was just happening.

Her body moved past me like breathtakingly beautiful scenery: the soft hollow of her throat, welted with what must have been bite-marks, the gorgeous sanctuary of her cleavage, still slick with sweat; her breasts physically caressing my eyes in passing; her belly, marred: the triple line of a scratch that I tried to kiss as it went by.

And then she opened her thighs just a little, closing them again, hot and wet, against my ears, sealing out most sounds and all thoughts, doubts, or fears.

I could just barely hear her tell me what a *good* boy I was, as I reverently did as I had been told.

**Excerpted from:**
**Jon Zelig's**
***The Heat***

### Chapter Four:  The Tests

"Well," she said, after seeming to savor that moment. "Perhaps it would be best if you spoke with Arkady Andreyevich himself."

The director of the clinic.

She tapped me on the shoulder, prompting me to stand, led me further down the corridor and ushered me into an office.

It could have been a 19$^{th}$ century study: three walls of bookshelves and dark wood, a massive desk with a green felt blotter; leather chairs and a sofa arrayed in front of the desk; but behind it, a floor-to-ceiling wall of dark glass, the woods behind the Skunkworks dimly visible, sepia tinted.

She sat me on the leather sofa, stroked my arm and then squeezed it.

"I *should* tell you that everything will be alright," she said sadly.  "But," without finishing the sentence, she swiveled on her impossibly high spike heels and strode from the room, the swish of the hem of her white coat against the pin-striped ass of her beautifully filled out pencil skirt, the light cloud of her perfume, sensory echoes that were almost instantly dispelled as the director of the medical clinic marched into the room.

With Viktor just on his heels.

I got hung up for a moment, wondering whether Viktor had held the door in respect, or followed as a demonstration of his utter indifference to symbols of power and protocol.

Not the point.

The director seated himself, facing me, behind his desk.

Viktor plopped down next to me on the sofa.

"Don't mind if I sit in?" he asked casually, his tag line whenever he crashed a meeting.

And who was ever going to tell the founder and CEO that they *did* mind?

Not me.

Certainly not today—though his presence, and the nurse's parting words, shot a spear of apprehension and terror through me that made me want to throw up.

Arkady Andreyevich—long white coat, a beard that belonged on George Bernard Shaw, a figure more out of Tolstoy than Post-Soviet Russia—steepled his fingers and began directly.

"They are not *side* effects," he said crisply. "They are *effects*. Intended, indeed," he allowed himself a tight little self-congratulatory smirk, "quite precisely *engineered* effects. Your wife is now . . . *painfully* beyond the scope of any easily obtained satisfaction. And you, well," it was possible that he felt some genuine regret about this, "you have simply lost the *capacity* to . . . *satisfy*."

He let this hang in the air, looking at me directly, gaze a little morose.

I looked down, unable, unwilling, to respond—though no response was really being required.

I'd been in automobile accidents, understood shock, the freezing of moments, suspension of time, and—for *me* at least—the intrusion of *ego.*

Before *this can't be happening,* I always went through something closer to: *Me? No. Surely you must mean someone else.*

But now . . .

What did I need to convince me?

*Facts had been stated.*

Having already been *graphically* demonstrated.

I looked briefly to my left.

Viktor's cold blue stare was terrifying; I held it for as long as I could.

Seconds?

*Why?*

And then . . . I gave up.

Because there was clearly nothing to do but give up.

It was a nightmare—I would, at some point, awaken—or it was reality.

It would somehow get better or—I tried to imagine how things could *possibly* get worse.

The dizziness was now almost overwhelming.

I'd had no alcohol for almost twenty-four hours—that single glass of wine at lunch the day before. And yet I felt on the precipice of sickening and incoherent drunkenness.

I held onto the dizziness—the smaller sickness a refuge from the tug of the greater fear.

"I *have* taken her," Viktor said softly, the mild observation of an established fact. "She knows or she does not. But. It is *done.* She has *The Heat,*" he said.

Which confused me for a moment.

*She was feverish?*

Yes. . .

127

Arkady Andreyevich murmured something in Russian and Viktor closed his eyes and nodded.

He spoke many languages and his technical English was without flaw. But sometimes it seemed that the noise in his head—and the grammar of his childhood—broke through and twisted his meaning.

"She is *in* heat," Viktor said, correcting himself, looking up again, fixing me in that lizard-like gaze. *"You know this. You know. If she doesn't yet, she will."*

I couldn't manage speech.

And there were only two words in my head anyway, booming with painful intensity, as though I were in a church tower—inside a church *bell*—as the clock chimed the hour.

*How?*

*Why?*

He turned away, reached to his left without looking and took a remote control from the end table next to him.

A fast flurry of button-pushing and two constellations of flat screen monitors—four each—unfolded from the ceiling in front of one of the bookcases.

"She knows nothing is accident," Viktor said amiably. "She *knows* this. But watch—*watch*," he urged me. "Watch what happens anyway. Yes, this is a test. But I know these tests; I know how they go. Lots of data," he murmured in satisfaction. "Good, *hard* data."

*Nothing is accident.*

Choice of words: not accident.

They had put her in what looked like a combined infirmary and exam room. Like everything else it was expensive and tastefully done: a medical facility designed by a luxury hotel purveyor. We had a multi-camera view of both the room and the attached bathroom. We had sound as well.

*I wanted to see this.*

*I desperately wanted not to see this.*

128

She was wearing a hospital gown, loose; it didn't look like there was anything underneath it.

There was an exam or procedure table on one side of the room, something more like a hospital bed on the other. The bed was made up, as in a hotel. Toward the foot of the bed, there was a bath towel on top of the covers, folded into a somewhat lumpy square.

She was pacing.

Arms folded across her chest, as if holding herself together, she walked the diagonal from corner to corner. Sometimes this was brisk and mechanical, at other times— with apparent difficulty—she held back, tried to maintain a more casual pace. But she couldn't make this last.

Breaking from that routine, she sat on the edge of the bed, knees together, hands on her thighs, leaning slightly, looking down at the floor, her legs rising and falling a little, as if she were riding a tiny invisible bicycle. She brought her hands to her knees, as if to still them; then put her elbows on her knees instead and lowered her face into her hands.

This seemed to calm her.

When she looked up again, glancing to her left, she saw the folded towel.

She stared at it for what felt like a long time.

Her legs went into motion again.

She stood, turned away from the bed, then back to the towel and leaned over. She slowly grasped a corner and lifted, as though raising a trophy fish in the air to be examined.

A foot-long wand vibrator fell out of the towel and landed on the bed. The top looked like a grey, rubber tennis ball; the handle was white plastic; a multi-setting switch was visible but not readable.

She picked it up.

My breath caught in my throat. I felt—it wasn't a *throb* because there was no blood, no inflation—I felt something like a longing, a *sting*, of imagined arousal and desire.

And fear.

Why fear?

"She'll *look* now," Viktor said softly, even as she furtively darted her eyes around the room.

But—expensive equipment, professionally installed—there was nothing for her to see.

"And now," Viktor said, "she can lie to herself—she has to—she can tell herself she is alone. She is not a stupid woman," he said, as if in wonder. "But she will pretend to believe in accidents—and invisibility—so she can do what she wants . . . well, what she *needs* to do."

She put the vibrator back down on the bed, handling it as though it were a small and delicate—or dangerous—animal. She stood for a moment, staring down at it, then walked to the door. She put her hand flat against it, as if this would tell her what was on the other side. She tried the knob, apparently for the first time, and discovered that the door was locked.

She blinked, frowned at this, then turned and walked slowly back to the bed.

Picking up the vibrator, she hefted it as though it were a police flashlight—half weapon—or a squash racquet—finely crafted and balanced—sat on the bed for a moment heavily, as if in resignation. Then she stood up, clasped the vibrator to her chest and walked briskly into the bathroom and closed the door.

Viktor did another quick finger ballet with the remote and the video screens all went dark.

The microphones stayed on, however.

"We give her *some* privacy," he said dryly.

We listened together—was it ten minutes? *fifteen?*—to a gorgeous but agonized symphony of arousal and frustration: the unmistakable spikes of climaxes that brought no end, no release, no relief; the crooning of pain

130

and pleasure and longing unsatisfied; a sobbing and wailing and crying out that the relentless rising and falling hum of the vibrator could not mask, still, or sate.

In the end there were only sobs.

There might have been words as well but I couldn't make them out.

And then the sound cut off and we sat in silence.

"So," Viktor said briskly, after giving the performance, and the restored quiet, some moments of respect. "As you can . . . *hear*, with no doubt. She has the—" he glanced briefly at the bearded doctor and then corrected himself. "She is *in* heat."

He nodded at his own conclusion.

"And I must help her," he said, without a trace of irony. "And," he said, his voice now colder, "I must, of course, help you as well."

There was a metal wastepaper basket to my right, just to the side of my end of the couch.

I threw up into it copiously, violently, and as neatly as I could manage.

I was on fire, instantly drenched in sweat; my head felt like it was about to explode.

And then I was simply *gone.*

**Excerpted from:**
**Jon Zelig's**
*The Heat*

131

# The Zelig Family

*Weird genetics? Something in the water? Odd family dynamics?* Whatever it is . . . The Zeligs *do* seem to be a little . . . erotically obsessed. But each one in their own particular way:

**Bram Zelig** skews toward Paranormal Romance & Erotica.

**Jon Zelig** does Femdom, often w/ elements of age play, cuckolding & male chastity.

**Joy Zelig**—Jon's twin and mirror image—does more Maledom.

**Zoë Zelig** is softer; BDSM, Maledom oriented, but more romantic, something of a *Fifty Shades of Grey*-inflected focus on wealth & power.

Their characters tend to love one another and they have an ongoing interest in the moral underpinnings of power exchange: What's consent, where are the lines, who gets to judge—sexually or emotionally? What's public and what's private? When do pain and pleasure shade into damage?

They're trying to do what we all try to do: just . . . make it work.

www.amazon.com/author/bramzelig
www.amazon.com/author/jonzelig
www.amazon.com/author/joyzelig
www.amazon.com/author/zoezelig

# Meet Jon Zelig!

Credit: Shutterstock

www.amazon.com/author/jonzelig

Jon Zelig writes about sexually intense, romantic, power exchange relationships: mostly Femdom—Maledom largely being the province of his twin sister Joy—often in conjunction with T&D, D&S, FLR, Chastity Play, and Cuckolding.

Age Play is a recurring theme: usually a *Wife-as-Dommy-Mommy*, disciplining and taking care of a *Bad-Little-Boy-Husband*.

In all of their work:

No "adult babies," no diapers, no cribs.

No incest, no violence, minimal compulsion.

More psychological domination than physical.

A bit of hand, hairbrush, or belt: no whips or crops or canes.

Pinked—or reddened—bottoms, backs, and thighs?
*Yes.*

Bleeding, bruising, *damage*?
*Dear, God(dess)!*
*No.*

Most of his work takes place in a contemporary setting: sometimes this is with an "alternative reality" skew; some is set in the near-term "Gynarchic Future."

Almost always—the intensity of the roles they are playing notwithstanding?—*The Zelig Twins'* characters love and try to take care of each other.
*Otherwise. . . ?*
What's the *point,* really?

jonzelig@anonymousspeech.com

# Work by Jon Zelig

The works itemized below are all available as ebooks; many are also available in paperback; a few as audiobooks.

E-Books on Amazon (where paperbacks, particularly of the full trilogies, are also available, as well as the audiobook versions), B&N, Smashwords, and all the places to which the latter "pushes out content." Some paperbacks also available via Lulu.

*Please* consider leaving a review on Amazon or Goodreads, or. . . wherever else you tend to post reviews.

See FREE ebook offer.

Finally, while I will trust that anything with "Femdom" or "Cuckolding" in the title pretty much explains itself, I have superscripted most of the work below to give some sense of "direction" and "orientation," using the following numbers as flags:

1. Femdom
2. Maledom
3. Mixed
4. Age Play
5. Lesbian Content
6. More Heavily Romantic
7. More "Intellectual," than Physical, Power Exchange
8. Paranormal Erotica
9. Elements of "Alternative Reality"

Novellas:

The Eight-Day Week: A Femdom Novella
The Heat: A Raw, Dystopian, Erotic, Love Story[6]
Protocols of the Sisterhood of the Gynarchy[9]

Collected Work:

Gynarchy Rising: Tales from a Femdom Future[9]
A Cuckolding Compendium
A Cuckolding Compendium, Volume II

Shorter Pieces:

Breathe: Lessons in CBT & Oral Submission[1]
Married, Chastised, Cucked, and Happy
The Serious Moonlight: A Cuckold Husband Tale[1]
They Say Payback's A—:
A Femdom Revenge Story[1,7]
Tipping: A Cuckold in Chastity Femdom Tale[1]

Serialized (or multi-volume) Novellas:

Series I[3]

Terms & Turns: Sex & Submission
Books I & II (duology)
Book I: Becoming a Good Boy[1]
    Audiobook
Book II: The Turn[2]
    Audiobook

Series II[1,7]

Beside Myself: The Full Trilogy
Book I: Drugged by His Femdom Wife
Book II: When It Rains, It Pours
Book III: The Fate of the Submissive Husband

Series III[9]

Lake Cuck-Amok: The Full Trilogy
Book I: A Role Retraining Resort
Book II: The Battle for Bob
Book III: Getting Right with The Gynarchy

Series IV[4]

Sold: A Triptych of Femdom Vignettes
Sold #1: A Femdom Vignette[1]
Sold #2: Celebrations & Choices
Sold #3: Where Does It Hurt?

Series V

The Man Whisperer Program:
Break Your Husband in 30 Days
The Full Trilogy
Book I: Dommy Mommy's Chaste Cuckold
Book II: Advanced Topics in
Successful Male Control
Book III: Or Your Money Back?

Series VI

Lose Your Wife in Three Easy Lessons
The Full Trilogy
Book I: The Master Cuckolded
Book II: A Matter of Judgment
Book III: Fighting for Jill

Series VII[3]

The Sexual Narratologist: The Full Trilogy
#1 Outsource Your Fantasies: Save Your Marriage!
#2 Calling Out the Wrong Name
#3 Two If by Night

Series VIII[3]

Punishment Incorporated: The Full Trilogy
Book I: Punishing the Succubus?
Book II: Mistress Judy's Journey
Book III: Tasha In Charge

Series IX

Cuckoldry Negotiated: The Full Trilogy
Book I: The Marriage Contract
Book II: Love & Honor & Obedience:
A Femdom Wedding Tale
Book III: A Femdom Honeymoon

Series X[9]

Internal Invasion & Erotic Evasion: The Full Trilogy
Book I: Terminal Orgasm
Book II: Battling for Inner Space
Book III: Subsumed

Series XI

Governess Dominates Couple: The Full Trilogy
Book I: The Fall into Her Thrall
Book II: Family Falls Further
Book III: After Fall, Spring?  No Spring

Series XII

Being Alessandra's, a D&S Romance:
The Full Trilogy
Book I: Home Is Where the Hurt Is
Book II: Hurting Each Other . . . Carefully
Book III: Where *Should* It Hurt?

Series XIII

Cuck-Tales for Three: The Full Trilogy
Book I: Tell Me a Sexy Story
Book II: Tipping into Cuckold Chastity
Book III: Finding the Right Cuckie-Sitter

Series XIV

A Femdom Age Play Journey
The Full Trilogy
Book I: Becoming Little Tommy
Book II: The New Rules
Book III: Bigger Badder Boys

Series XV

A Loss of Sexual Control:
Cuck Desires & Wifely Needs
The Full Trilogy
Book I: Lock Me Out Lock Me In
Book II: Bringing Home the Reality
Book III: *Can* You Go Home Again?

Series XVI

Femdom Wife Takes Control
The Full Trilogy
Book I: You Put a Chip, Where?!
Book II: Teaching Lessons & Learning Rules
Book III: Too Far?

Series XVII (in progress)

Double-Cucked & Regressed
The Full Trilogy
Book I: Meeting the Bull-Breaker
Book II: Back to School
Book III: (forthcoming)

Series XVIII (in progress)

The Cuckold Clinic
The Full Trilogy
Book I: Faking It
Book II: The Pleasure of Terror
Book III: (forthcoming)

Series IXX (in progress)[1,5,8,9]

Sex & Santería: The Full Trilogy
Book I: Submitting to The Priestess Next Door
Book II: (forthcoming)
Book III: (forthcoming)

# Connect with Jon Zelig

Deeply impressed (and grateful) that you "made it all the way through." *Thank You!* Hope you enjoyed the trip. Questions, comments, complains, suggestions, rants, or screeds?

Contact: jonzelig@anonymousspeech.com

*—JZ*

Wordpress: https://zeligmedia.wordpress.com/
Goodreads: http://tinyurl.com/hyxejkx
Librarything: http://tinyurl.com/hetaars
Pinterest: http://tinyurl.com/zatbvs8

Email List Sign Up:

**http://eepurl.com/cKUGov**

# Meet *Joy* Zelig!

Credit: Shutterstock

www.amazon.com/author/joyzelig

Jon Zelig's work is largely focused on Femdom Erotica.

His, *five-minutes-younger* twin sister, tends more in the direction of Maledom, somewhat in parallel—or perhaps in mirror image: a *Dommy-Daddy-Husband*, with *a Bratty-Adolescent-Wife*, as in her *Yes, No, Maybe Trilogy.*

The *JZ Twins* also do a bit of *Sloshing Across Lines*, some of their work tending to do "a little of both" or not being easily fit into either—or perhaps *any!*—category.

joyzelig@anonymousspeech.com

# Work by *Joy* Zelig

Available, or forthcoming, in the Kindle Store.
*Please* consider leaving a review on Amazon, or. . .
wherever else you tend to post reviews.


Collected Work:

A Maledom Anthology:
Stories of Sexually Surrendered Women
A Maledom Punishment Primer

Shorter Pieces:

Chemical Accidents: An Age Play Tale
Taking It: Too Big for the Size Queen?
A Backdoor Erotic Romance: Where Does Love Go?

Serialized (or multi-volume) Novellas:

Series I

Yes, No, Maybe? A Trilogy of Age Play Novellas
    Audiobook
Book I: Yes, Daddy: An Age Play Novella
Book II: No, Wifey: An Age Play Novella
Book III: Maybe, We. . . ?: An Age Play Novella

Series II

The Good Master: The Full Trilogy
    Audiobook
Book I: Losing Darla
Book II: Darla's Gift
Book III: A Matter of Grace

Series III

Sexual Manners at The Manor
The Full Trilogy
Book I: Lola and Angelique's Punishment
Book II: Occupied by an Erotic Army
Book III: Chasing Out the Sexual Psychopaths

Series IV

Consent & Desire & Submission
The Full Trilogy
Book I: A Psycho-Sexual Cascade
Book II: An Honorable Sexual Surrender
Book III: A Sexual Reckoning

Series V

The Reverend's Wife Debauched
The Full Trilogy
Book I: Jezebel Falling
Book II: Jezebel's Paradise of Pain
Book III: Jezebel Rising

Series VI

A Bisexual Femdom Romance
The Full Trilogy
Book I: Grace: *Pressured*
Book II: Finn: *Falling*
Book III: Grace: *Rising*

# Meet Bram Zelig!

Credit: Shutterstock

www.amazon.com/author/bramzelig

Bram Zelig—a cousin of the, erotica-writing, twins Jon Zelig & Joy Zelig, the former more Femdom-Focused, the latter more Maledom-Oriented—writes about the supernatural in a contemporary setting, erotica and romance threading through the tapestry of his work.

Vampires walk among us, thirsty for blood! And . . . sometimes hungry for love, sex, and a little compassion. Just because you have "biting issues" doesn't mean you're fundamentally bad! Just because you're supernaturally attractive, charming, and magnetic doesn't make you *good*—or necessarily the best person to get into a relationship with!

And . . . just because Love, Sex, Death (and *The Undead*) are serious topics?  Doesn't mean there's never anything to laugh about. *Otherwise. . . ?*  What's the *point, really?*

bramzelig@protonmail.com

# Work by Bram Zelig

Sister No More an Erotic Vampire Romance

The Corie Chronicles: Trilogy #1

Book I: Tears of Blood
Book II: The Truth *Won't* Set You Free
Book III: Family Sacrifices

# Meet Zoë Zelig!

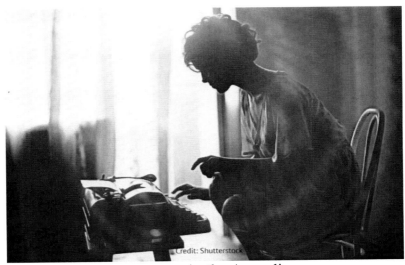

Credit: Shutterstock

www.amazon.com/author/zoezelig

*Zoë Zelig* read all the FSOG books, can't let go of them, remains obsessed with dominant rich men whose appetites combine romance with erotic discipline and the strong women who are moths to the flame: desperate for love, drawn to men who provide the right elixir: love, pain, pleasure, freedom, structure, support.

zoezelig@protonmail.com

# Work by Zoë Zelig

Tales from a Long Island Dungeon: A BDSM Romance

The Jason Flood Chronicles: Trilogy #1

Book I: A Diamond in the Rough
Book II: The Scent of Surrender
Book III: Coming to Terms

# The Zelig Family E-Mail List

Sign up; get a free PDF of Jon Zelig's *The Heat: A Raw, Dystopian, Erotic, Love Story.*

Receive periodic updates, bonuses, and freebies from Jon, Joy, Bram, and Zöe Zelig.

Your email address will NEVER be revealed, loaned, given, or sold to *any-other-entity* EVER.

Sign up here: http://eepurl.com/cKUGov

Let me know: jonzelig@anonymousspeech.com

I'll send the free book.

Thanks!

JZ

# Write a Review:
# Get a FREE eBook!

Review anything by Jon, Joy, or Bram Zelig, send me a link:

## jonzelig@anonymousspeech.com

Let me know which book, listed below, you are interested in.

**Jon Zelig:**

Sold #1: A Femdom Vignette

They Say Payback's A—: A Femdom Revenge Story

To Love, Honor, and Obey: A Femdom Wedding Tale

**Joy Zelig:** ¶

Chemical Accidents: An Age Play Tale
The Good Master, Book I: Losing Darla

Yes, Daddy: An Age Play Novella

**Bram Zelig:**

Sister No More, an Erotic Vampire Romance, Book II: The Truth *Won't* Set You Free

**Zöe Zelig:**

Tales from a Long Island Dungeon: A BDSM Romance (The Jason Flood Chronicles: Trilogy #1)

**Email List Sign Up: http://eepurl.com/cKUGov**

# Reviews

**Jon Zelig's Work:**

Punishment Incorporated: The Full Trilogy

Cuckoldry Negotiated: The Marriage Contract

Protocols of the Sisterhood of the Gynarchy

Lose Your Wife in Three Easy Lessons: The Full Trilogy

Submitting to the Priestess Next Door

Cuckoldry Negotiated: The Full Trilogy

**Joy Zelig's Work:**

Yes, No, Maybe: A Trilogy of Age Play Novellas

The Good Master: The Full Trilogy

**Bram Zelig's Work:**

Sister No More: The Full Trilogy

*REV23SEP17*

Made in United States
North Haven, CT
02 February 2025

65271698R00109